GILBERT
MAGNETIC FUN AND FACTS

WRITTEN BY
A. C. GILBERT, M. D.
AND
H. D. STONE, A. B.

Associate Member American Society of Mechanical
Engineers, Associate Member American
Society of Electrical Engineers

Published by

THE A. C. GILBERT COMPANY
NEW HAVEN, CONN.

New York   Chicago   San Francisco   Toronto   London

FOREWORD

Magnetism has always seemed to me to be such a fascinating subject, — it affects our everyday life so greatly that I thought those boys who are interested in Gilbert Toys would like to know more about it. So I have endeavored to compile information on magnetism in many of its forms that will be interesting for you to know. A thorough study of this book will, I am sure, give you a much better understanding of what magnetism means to all of us.

The boy who knows about different kinds of engineering —electrical, chemical, structural, etc.—the kinds that are covered by Gilbert Toys, is the type of a boy who will be a leader among his fellow boy friends. He is the boy whom the rest of the boys look up to, and they only do it because they appreciate that he has a knowledge of different things which they don't understand.

You can be a leader among your boy friends and you won't have to study and work hard to become one either. You don't have to do that at all. You can get all kinds of interesting information about sciences and other things right while you are playing. This book is only one of many of its kind that I have had compiled. Used in conjunction with the Gilbert Toys they describe, they offer you the best kind of an opportunity to have all kinds of fun and at the same time put you up among the leaders of boys.

Sincerely yours,

A. C. Gilbert

TABLE OF CONTENTS

GILBERT
MAGNETIC FUN AND FACTS

Chapter I

A SEA FOG

Have you ever been sailing in a boat way out at sea when the fog came down about you so that you could not see one end of the boat from the other? How did the captain guide the vessel toward port? He had one little thing to help him keep his course. That was the ship's compass.

Perhaps some of you have been hiking in the woods at night when the rain or clouds prevented the stars from shining. How did you find your way through the woods back to camp? If you had not the sense of direction, you probably used a compass to keep you from getting lost.

Did you know that this simple compass is one of the first magnets discovered? Men have found various other magnets after long years of search and have gradually learned how to use them. Today ships not only are guided through the fog, but are also lighted by electric lights, signals sent across the ocean, elevators run, bread baked and numberless other things done by the help of magnets.

Suppose we go back to the very beginning of these discoveries and, by making experiments, learn all we can about magnetism.

Sometime during the first hundred years A. D., wide-awake men and boys living around Magnesia, which is a town in Asia Minor, found pieces of hard, black stone which would pull or attract iron to them or would be pulled or attracted to the iron itself. Probably the first man to discover this found little pieces of this black stone clinging to the iron tip of his travelling staff

5

which all the wayfarers used in those days. This peculiar black stone is found in several places in the world and is a kind of iron ore.

Perhaps you remember the story of the Arabian Nights about the wonderful iron mountain against which ships were pulled and dashed to pieces. Evidently the writer had heard of this wonderful iron stone and must have believed that the mountain was made of it.

A long time afterward, some unknown man discovered that if you hung one of these black stones on a thread or made a raft of cork or wood and laid the stone floating in a basin of water, a wonderful thing happened. The stone turned and pointed nearly north and south! The Chinese found this out perhaps sooner than the Europeans and put this peculiar quality to work as the earliest form of compasses on their sailing vessels. Before this time, men had to depend entirely upon the sun and stars, and if a fog came up or a night was cloudy, they lost their way and were often wrecked.

Men familiar with minerals have given this iron ore the name of "magnetite" which you see sounds very much like "magnet". Sailors who used these stones for guidance over the seas called them "lodestones", which in those days meant the same as "leading

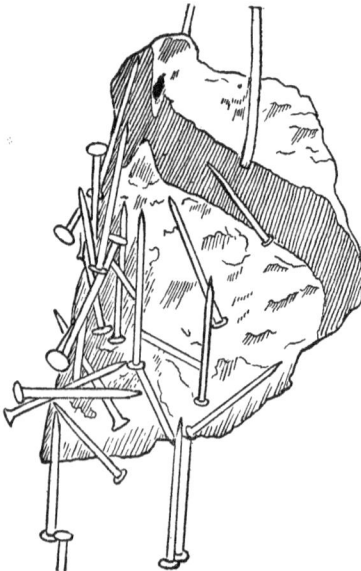

FIG. 1

stone". Figure 1 shows a picture of one of these natural magnets or lodestones with iron nails clinging to it.

The next important discovery in this line was that hard iron or steel rubbed on these natural magnets became permanently magnetized and would draw other pieces of iron or steel to them.

The first reliable book on magnetism was written by Dr. Gilbert, an Englishman, in about 1600 A. D. Let us start with Dr. Gilbert's experiments and learn first about the compass.

THE COMPASS

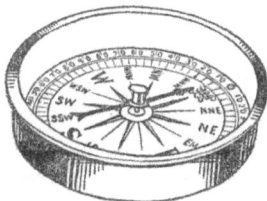

FIG. 2

Figure 2 is a picture of a compass. Notice first the black needle swinging on the pivot. Which way does the needle try to point? One end will try to point north and the other end turns toward the south. Around the bottom of the case is a paper with the different points of the compass marked. This paper is commonly called the wind-sail. See Figure 3.

FIG. 3

BOY SCOUTS, in order to become second class scouts, learn the sixteen principal points of the compass, and, in reciting them, do what sailors call "boxing the compass". The list given below covers all points of the compass and the numbered points, those you are required to know to pass the SECOND CLASS SCOUT TEST.

(1) North
    North by east
(2) North, north-east
    North-east by north

(3) North-east
    North-east by east
(4) East, north-east
    East by north

(5) East
    East by south
(6) East, south-east
    South-east by east
(7) South-east
    South-east by south
(8) South, south-east
    South by east
(9) South
    South by west
(10) South, south-west
    South-west by south

(11) South-west
    South-west by west
(12) West, south-west
    West by south
(13) West
    West by north
(14) West, north-west
    North-west by west
(15) North-west
    North-west by north
(16) North, north-west
    North by west
    North

Spin the needle around and notice that it comes back to rest always pointing in the same direction. Tie a little thread about the middle of a bar magnet and you will see that, when it comes to rest, it also points nearly north and south. Take a horseshoe magnet and hang it up by the top so that the shiny ends are toward the ground and the end with the mark on it will point nearly toward the north. Why do they all act this way?

FIG. 4

Dr. Gilbert proved that this earth we live in is a great magnet. He found that this natural magnet had two ends or poles, one in the very northern part of North America and the other in the Antarctic regions. These draw the ends of all other magnets toward them. This is the reason why the magnet needle always tries to point north and south, but remember that the north and south poles spoken of in geography are at different locations from these. The compass really points not true north and south but rather to these magnetic places. The angle between the direct north and south line and the direction in which all compasses point is called the DECLINATION and varies at different places.

Figure 4 shows a map of the magnetic lines going toward the North Magnetic Pole. A compass placed in any one of these lines will point as shown by the arrows.

MAKING A MAGNET

Suppose we take a sewing needle and a piece of soft iron wire. Touch the point of the needle to one end of the iron wire. What happens? Nothing happens, and the needle can be removed without trouble. Why? It is because the steel of the needle has not been magnetized. Rub the point of the needle on one end of the horseshoe magnet and again touch one of the iron wires. You will see that the wire sticks to the point of the needle and tries to hang on when you move the needle.

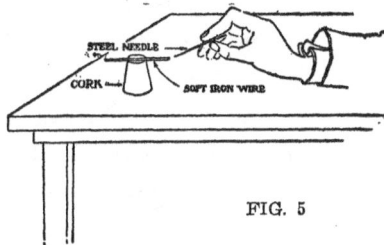

FIG. 5

In Figure 5 you will see another way to make this experiment by laying the soft iron wire on top of a cork and holding your needle against an end of the wire. The first time, before the steel is magnetized, nothing happens. The second time the iron wire seems to jump to the steel needle and clings so that you can pull it off the cork.

These experiments prove to us that a piece of steel or hard iron can be magnetized not only by rubbing it against a lodestone but also by rubbing it against the end of *any* magnet.

Take another needle and, before magnetizing it, suspend it by a thread so that it hangs level. Now touch one end with an end of a magnet. What happens? If you live north of the equator, the north-pointing end of the needle drops downward. If south of the equator, the south-pointing end of the needle points down. How can we explain this?

Dr. Gilbert found this to be caused by the pull of the earth's magnetism. It has been proven that, as we go further north, the pull of the North Magnetic Pole makes the needle point more and more downward until we have reached the very spot of the magnetic pole itself when the needle will point straight down. In the same way going south of the equator, we find the needle dipping more and more until the South Magnetic Pole is reached. See Figure 6.

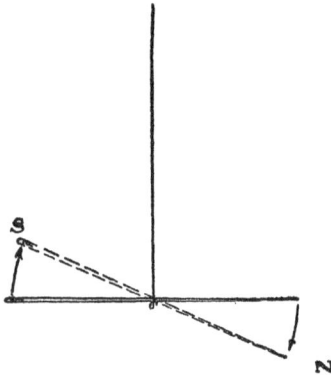

FIG. 6

Inclination—The needle hangs parallel with the floor before magnetized. After magnetization it dips. North of the equator the dip is shown by the dotted lines.

This curious thing is known as the MAGNETIC INCLINATION. For some reason yet unknown, both the magnetic inclination and declination vary from time to time. One variation is every eleven years; another every time there is an eclipse of the sun.

POLARITY

Pour some iron filings on a paper and drop a bar magnet in them as shown in Figure 7. What happens?

You will see the little specks of iron form themselves together in little hairs or whiskers and jump and cling to the ends of the bar magnet, but in the middle part of the magnet there are practically no iron filings. This shows that the mysterious magnetic force is stronger at the ends or points of the magnet and apparently has little or no force in the middle. Dr. Gilbert called the ends of the magnet the POLES. The one turning toward the north he called the north pole; the one turning toward the south, the south pole.

FIG. 7

By experimenting with little soft iron wires, you will find that NON-MAGNETIZED IRON OR STEEL WILL ATTRACT EITHER POLE OF A MAGNET.

Look at a bar magnet. You will notice one end is usually marked with an "N" or with a "+" sign. Hold one end toward the suspended needle as in Figure 8. What happens? One end of your sewing needle turns toward the bar magnet and tries to stick to it. Hold the same end of your bar magnet toward the other end of your needle. What happens? It doesn't attract, does it? It seems to try to get away. What does this mean? Turn the bar magnet around in your hand and hold the other end of it toward the ends of the needle. What happens now? You will find the end that was

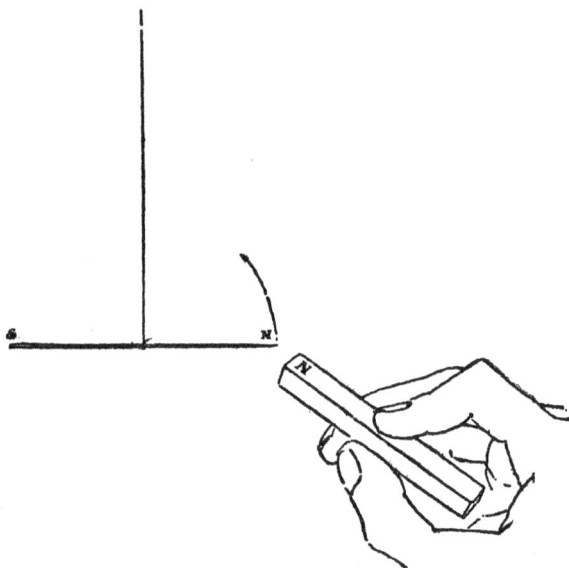

FIG. 8

pulled toward the bar magnet before now turns away while the other end comes rushing around to grab the other end of the bar.

Hang up one bar magnet in the same way and hold another bar magnet toward it. See Figure 9. You will find the two act toward each other just as the needle and magnet did, and, if you will look closely, you will find that the ends marked "N" push each other away and if you hold an "N" end toward the plain end of the other bar magnet, they pull toward each other.

Another interesting way to try this experiment is to lay one bar magnet on the table, as in Figure 10, balance another on top of it, giving the top one a little push, and you will see that it will swing so that the marked end of it is at the opposite end from the marked end of the bottom one.

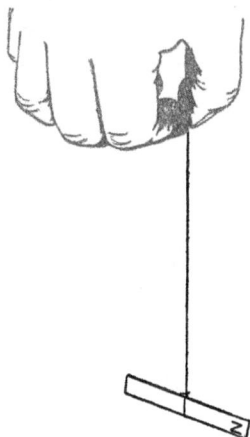

All these experiments prove to us that magnets not only attract each other, but repel and further than this, the NORTH-SEEKING ENDS REPEL EACH OTHER AND THE SOUTH-SEEKING ENDS REPEL EACH OTHER, but a SOUTH END WILL ATTRACT A NORTH END and likewise a NORTH END, A SOUTH END. The ENDS of the magnet are called POLES and the discovery above

FIG. 9

is made into a statement or law which says "LIKE POLES REPEL EACH OTHER; UNLIKE POLES ATTRACT."

Now we must ask ourselves, what is magnetism? That is yet to be found out. No one knows just what it is, neither do they know what electricity is. Currents of electricity and magnetism always seem to be found together and the men of electrical science have put this pair of giants to work as their servants in a great many different ways, sometimes making magnetism work to increase the power of electricity, other times making electric currents work to increase the magnetic forces.

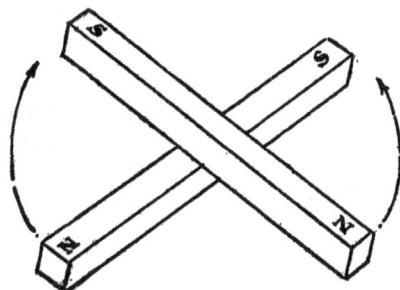

FIG. 10

WHERE MAGNETISM IS

This leads us to wonder where these magnetic forces may be found and though we do not know what it is, a great deal is known of the "Fields" through which the force of magnetism acts and along what "Lines" these forces go.

FIG. 11

Floating Needle and Bar Magnet. Small Needles Can Be Laid Gently on the Surface of Water and Will Float.

Try this experiment to prove it. Take a bar magnet. Lay it on the table on top of a piece of writing paper. Move a compass,

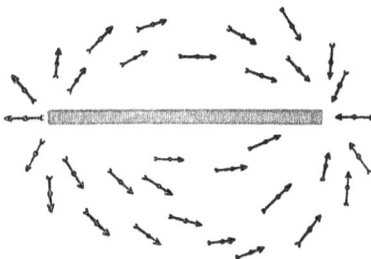

FIG. 12

starting at one pole of the magnet, gradually toward the other pole, stopping at distances equal to a little more than the length of the compass needle. Let the compass needle come to rest in each place and when we have noticed the position it takes, draw a picture of this position on the piece of paper as in Figure 12. Notice how the picture seems to make long, circular lines reaching from one pole to the other, crowded together at the poles and spreading apart at a position halfway between the poles.

These lines gave the earlier discoverers of magnetic power the idea of calling them LINES OF FORCE and, after drawing this picture, can we not easily imagine these magnetic lines of force spreading out in all directions from the pole tips? Yes, they spread IN ALL directions.

You will find this is true if you take your magnetized sewing needle suspended by a little thread at its middle and hold it over the magnet from the north to the south pole, you will see the dip of the needle changes. If you set a paper up back of the needle and draw these changes, you would see a line coming up in the air just the same as those made by the compass on the flat piece of paper. See Figure 13.

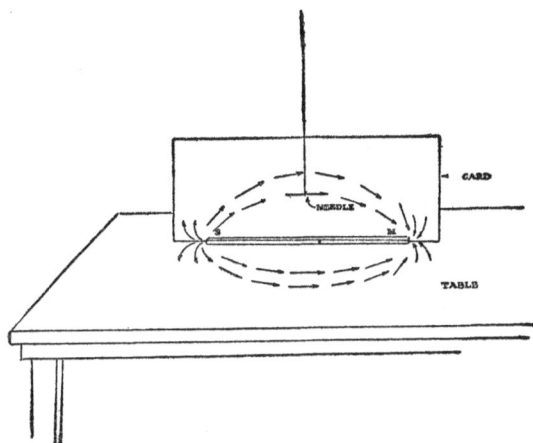

FIG. 13

Let us take the iron filings again. Sprinkle them on a piece of cardboard or glass and place the bar magnet under it. By tapping the glass gently, the iron filings will arrange themselves in lines starting from one pole and circling around towards the other pole.

Try a horseshoe magnet and you will find lines crowding between the north and south poles, some starting up in the air and some swerving in large circles from the north and south poles. This should tell us that most of the magnetic lines seek the shortest distance between the poles, crowding just as many lines as possible in the space. The remaining lines swing out and occupy the next available space on their journey toward the opposite pole. See Figures 14 and 15.

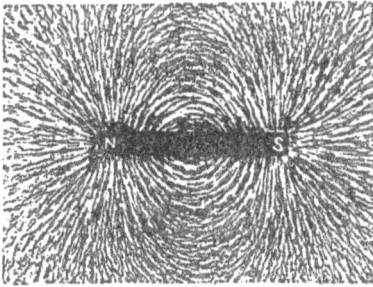

FIG. 14

Now that this experiment has been performed, some of us will think that if we sprinkle the filings on the glass over two north or south poles, which are near together, we should see the lines repel each other. Put your two bar magnets under the glass and sprinkle filings on top and you will surely see this wonderful result. See Figure 16.

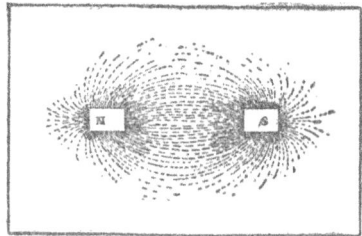

FIG. 15

Another curious thing about a magnet is that if you break one in the middle you will still have north and south poles. Take one of the magnetized needles and break it in half. Hold one of the broken pieces toward the compass. What happens? In agreement with the rules noted above, the north pole of the compass needle is attracted by the south pole of the broken needle. Should you break it again, you would find that the broken piece has north and south

B—1

poles which attract or repel the compass needle according to whether you hold unlike or like poles toward each other.

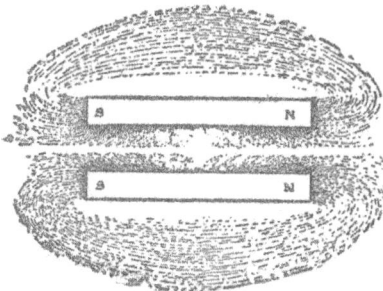

FIG. 16

Figure 17 shows a magnet broken twice and if we could break it into the smallest pieces, each little piece would still have its north and south poles. In fact, one theory in regard to magnetism is that the little pieces or molecules of metal in any piece of iron or steel, in becoming magnetized, try to push with one end toward the north and the other end toward the south.

KINDS OF MAGNETS

There are two kinds of permanent magnets, the bar and the horseshoe magnet, Figure 18. These are the two most common artificial magnets and they are al-

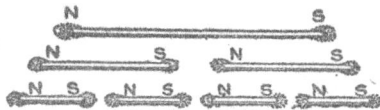

FIG. 17

so known as permanent magnets because they hold magnetism for a long time. The horseshoe magnet will lift three or four times as much as a bar magnet and is the strongest permanent magnet in use. When it is necessary to get a stronger pull than these will give, an electro magnet is used which we will study later.

FIG. 18
Bar Magnet and Horseshoe Magnet Made Up of Thin Strips Fastened Together.

B — 2

MAGNETIC MATERIALS

So far we have been talking about iron and steel and lodestones, but have not considered any other materials. As good scientists, we ought to discover whether any other things can be attracted or repelled, so let us try a few experiments.

Take a piece of copper. Does it stick to the magnet? Try brass, wood, paper, fibre, cloth. If you make a list, you will find iron and steel are the only common materials which magnetism will move. Cobalt and nickel are also attracted by magnets.

There are a few substances such as bismuth, antimony phosphorus which are called DIA-MAGNETIC because they apparently are repelled from both of the magnet poles, but it is not possible for us to experiment with these so we will content ourselves with more common materials and substances.

Hold an end of one of your bar magnets near a steel ball. You will find there is attraction for both the north and south poles. This seems to dispute the statement that "Like poles repel and unlike poles attract". It is caused by the ball being round; therefore having no points or poles. MAGNETIC SUBSTANCES WITHOUT POLES ALWAYS ATTRACT EITHER POLE OF A MAGNET.

MAGNETIC INDUCTION

Let us take a small piece of glass and sprinkle iron filings on top of it. Hold the glass up and place a bar magnet underneath it. What happens? The little iron filings jump into curious forms piling up on top of each other, others forming together in lines running from one pole of the magnet to the other. Repeat this experiment using a horseshoe magnet, and again you will see the little fellows piling up in long strings. Hold the horseshoe magnet against a bottle full of iron wire or iron filings and you can lift it from the table without touching it with your hands. Put iron filings on a piece of cardboard or paper and your magnet underneath. What happens? The magnetism has its effect through the glass or paper each time. Repeat this experiment with other materials.

We find that magnetism is forced through all the non-magnetic materials, but if we take a tin cup or iron dish and pour some of the iron filings on it, holding the magnet underneath, there is no effect. We can then say that magnetic material acts as a shield against the passage of magnetism, but non-magnetic material offers little resistance to magnetic force.

This is good to remember when you carry a watch near any electric machinery or on the street cars. The best way to keep your watch from having its spring magnetized is to enclose it in a soft iron case. Some people use a hard rubber case but we have already found, by experiment, that this is non-magnetic, and, therefore, does not stop the force of magnetism.

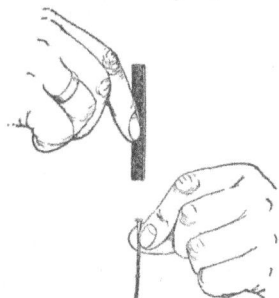

One more experiment is to take a bar magnet and with the other hand hold a piece of iron wire near one of the poles of the magnet, being careful not to touch it, as shown in Figure 19. Touch the end of the iron wire to one of the other little

FIG. 19

pieces of iron wire and see what happens. We have discovered that the first iron wire has the power to attract the second wire to it, but if the magnet is removed, the second wire will soon fall off. We have learned two new things. First, that a magnet may make unmagnetic things strongly magnetized. This is done through non-magnetic material, and is called INDUCTION. We have also found that some magnetic material loses its magnetism very easily. By experiment, we find that soft iron will not hold magnetism, but hard iron, and especially hard steel, will remain magnetic for years. If you try scratching a magnet, you will notice that it is very hard in comparison with iron wires, screws, etc.

The magnetism of the greatest magnet of all, the earth, will convert, by induction, any piece of iron or steel into a magnet. Almost all the iron and steel framework of buildings and bridges around you are magnetized. Steel ships are so strongly magnetic that they influence the magnetic needles of their compasses so much that every little while the compasses have to be adjusted, and, in adjusting, they are protected from the ship's magnetism by means of balls of soft iron placed in such a position around the compass that it neutralizes these outside magnetic forces.

TERRESTRIAL INDUCTION

An interesting experiment to further illustrate the preceding paragraph can be made with a piece of iron; for example, an ordinary stove poker. If you hold it in a horizontal position, pointing east and west, generally both ends will attract either end of the compass needle, showing that the poker has not yet become polarized; but if you hold it in a north-south direction and bring the needle near one end you will notice from the direction of the needle that the poker has become magnetized with distinct north and south poles, for it will repel the north pole of the compass at one end and attract it at the other. If you turn the poker in the east-west position again both ends will attract the same end of the compass needle, showing that it is again non-magnetic. To increase the

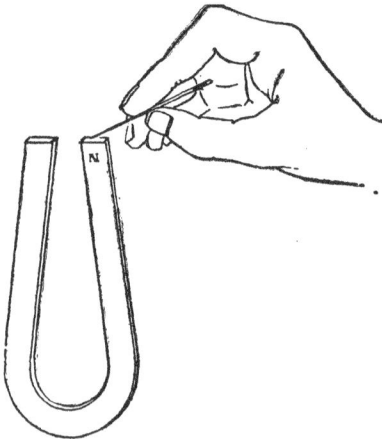

FIG. 20
Single Touch Method

effects of the induced action of the earth hold the poker north-south

again and give it a few sharp blows with a hammer. This shakes its molecules and enables the induced force of the earth's magnetism to turn them more easily in north-south position. By again exploring with your compass you will find that the poker has become permanently magnetized. To de-magnetize it hold it in an east-west position and hit it a few sharp blows again.

METHODS OF MAKING MAGNETS

There are three principal methods of making permanent magnets. The first is by single touch, Figure 20. This is what we did in magnetizing our sewing needles when we stroked one pole of our magnet with one end of the needle.

The second method is called the double touch and

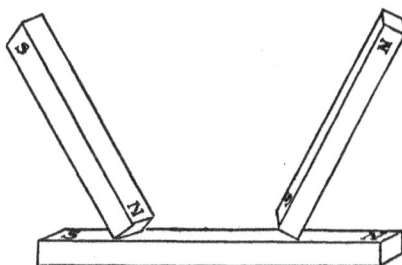

DOUBLE TOUCH

FIG. 21A

by it we can magnetize two new magnets at a time holding the ends as shown in Figure 21A, rubbing them along the magnet until they reach the poles. The third method is called the divided touch and is very much like the second

DIVIDED TOUCH

FIG. 21B

except that at the start the two new magnets are not touched together but are carefully separated by a piece of cork, paper, wood, or other non-magnetic material. See Figure 21B.

We will discuss, a little later, a better method than any of these which will require currents of electricity.

HEAT AND MAGNETISM

Magnets lose their magnetism if they are handled roughly or if they are heated too much. A magnetized sewing needle can be de-magnetized by heating it red-hot. An interesting experiment can be made by bending an iron wire in the form of a circle or by using a thin metal disc supported, as shown in Figure 22, in front of a horseshoe magnet. By placing a flame under one side of the iron ring, the ring will begin to turn. This happens because the heated parts are not affected by the magnetic force while the cool parts are attracted. Therefore, the cool section moves forward. If we place the lamp or candle directly in front of the horseshoe magnet, as shown in Figure 22, we can make the ring revolve as long as the flame heats the iron.

FIG. 22

Chapter II

ELECTRO-MAGNETISM

Now that we have gone through the history of Dr. Gilbert's wonderful discoveries, let us pay a visit to Copenhagen, to the laboratory of Mr. Oersted. We are now in the year 1819 when people are just beginning to hear of steamboats and steam trains and have no electric cars, electric lights, telephones or telegraph. We arrive just in time to find our friend, Mr. Oersted, greatly excited. He asks us to place a sewing needle in a cork with the sharp end sticking straight upwards, putting the compass needle on its point.

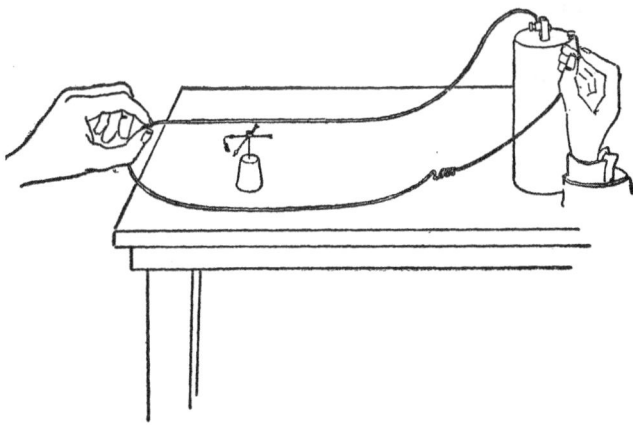

FIG. 23

We are next instructed to attach a copper wire to the middle terminal post of a battery and hold the other end of the wire in our hand, being sure that both ends of this wire are scraped bright and clean. Hold the wire over the needle, as in Figure 23, so that it runs in a straight line in the same direction as the needle is pointing and, with the free end of the wire, touch the outside terminal post of the battery. If the wire is close to the magnetic needle, what do we see? The needle immediately swings around as if some magnetic force is pulling it.

In the study of batteries, we find that the middle binding post is called positive or "+" and the electric current passes out from it toward the outside terminal post which is called negative or "—". If you hold this wire over the compass in such a way that the current flows from south to north, what direction does the north end of the compass needle point? I say "West" and you will find this to be correct.

To remember this, think of the word "Snow". The letters of this word are explained as follows: S—South, N—North, O—Over, turns W—West.

Now Mr. Oersted asks us to hold the wire in the same position

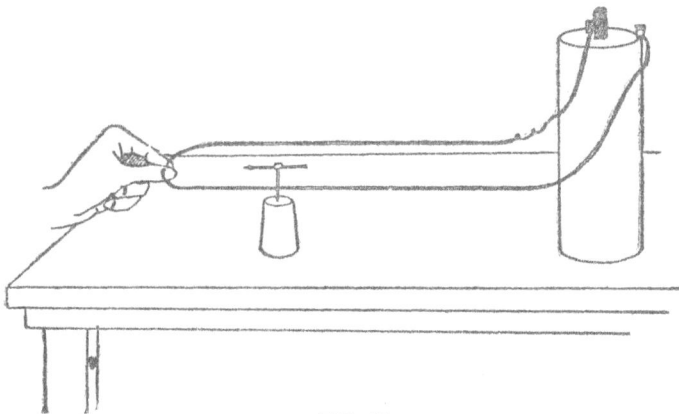

FIG. 24

but under the needle and we find—what? You are ready to say that the needle turns in the opposite direction. This must be due to the current, because when we no longer touch the outside binding post of the battery, the compass swings back to its north and south position.

Later another great scientist, Mr. Ampere, made the following rule by which we can remember which way a flow of current in a wire will affect a magnet needle. "Suppose a man swimming in the wire with the current, always facing the needle, then the N—seeking pole of the needle will be deflected toward his left hand." This discovery of our friend Oersted is one of the greatest steps in the marvelous development in electricity of today. It proves that around electrical current there is a magnetic force acting in accordance with the direction of flow of current.

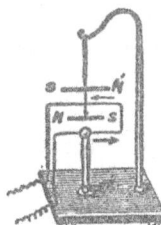

Place a loop of wire around the needle in such a way that the top of the loop is directly over the bottom part, as shown in Figure 24.

FIG. 25

Send a current through the loop from the battery and note the movement of the needle.

A greater turning effect of the needle is obtained by combining the force of the current flowing above the needle with the force flowing below, as shown in Figure 25.

The compass needle swings at right angles to the wire, as far as you can tell. Larger needles can not swing quite at right angles because the earth's magnetism is pulling them as well as the force caused by the electric current. Is there any way to overcome this?

Suspend a bar magnet on a thread and, about an inch below, another bar magnet with its north pole directly under the top magnet's south pole. See Figure 25. If these two bar magnets are of equal strength, they no longer point north and south and you can turn them in any direction. This is due to the fact that we have the magnets opposing and acting on each other just as two teams of men in a tug-of-war act. If both teams pull at the same time with equal strength

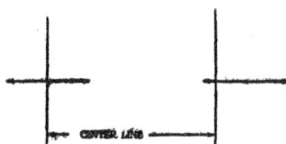

CENTER LINE

FIG. 26

on a rope, the rope does not move, but when one team pulls harder than the other the rope moves toward the direction in which there is the strongest pull. See Figure 26.

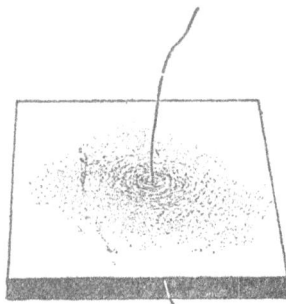

FIG. 27

When we have made the two magnets neutralize the pull of the earth's magnetism, we have then obtained a device which is affected entirely by the current flowing through the wire. We can make an instrument from this for measuring   the   flow   of   electricity. When one magnet is placed near the other so that together they neutralize the effect of the earth's magnetism, we say they are "astatic."

MAGNETIC FORCE ABOUT A WIRE

Push a copper or brass wire through the center of a cardboard. The latter should be about as large as a playing card. Connect the bare ends of the wire to a battery. One dry cell will do, but two or more will give a much better effect. After the current has started to flow, drop a few iron filings on the cardboard as near to the wire as possible. What happens?

Figure 27 shows how the results of this experiment will look. The iron filings arrange themselves in little rings thicker and closer together near the wire and thinner as they go farther away. Remembering what we found about the way which the current flows in the battery, we find by putting the compass around the wire in various places, that these magnetic circles flow one way when the current from the battery goes up the wire, the opposite way when it goes down.

WIRE WITH CURRENT COMING UP.

FIG. 28

Figure 28 shows what occurs when the current flows up the wire. The north pole of the magnetism goes around opposite from the way the hands of clock go. If the current in the wire flows down, the polarity goes around in the same direction as the hands of the clock. Try the compass needle in different positions around the wire and note that the magnetism always whirls around at right angles to the wire.

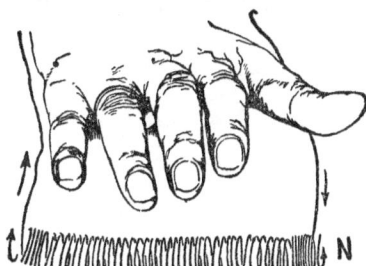

FIG. 29

We have found what happens on a straight wire, now try a crooked wire in form of a spring as shown in Figure 29.

Make the coil large enough to go through a piece of cardboard as in Figure 30, then try again with iron filings or the compass. The result is similar to that produced by a bar magnet.   Magnetism around single loops of wire act upon each other to form the magnetic forces shown in Figure 31.

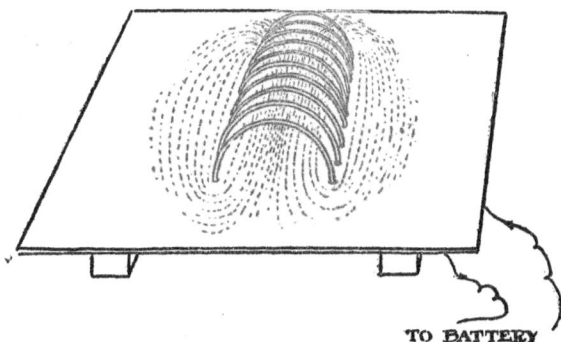

TO BATTERY

FIG. 30

You will also find that the current flowing in the wire as shown in Figure 32 will set up the north pole on the end marked "N". A good way to remember this is to hold your right hand, as shown in the picture, with the thumb sticking out at right angles from the fingers.   If the fingers are closed around the coil pointing in the direction in which the current is flowing, the thumb will point

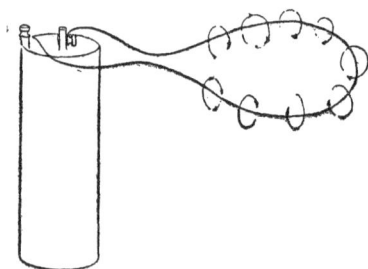

FIG. 31

toward the north pole. If you suspend this coil so that it can turn freely and yet be connected to the battery, you will find it points north and south just as your compass did and two coils near each other with the current flowing in them attract and repel each other.

Attach the ends of two coils of wire to each other and to a battery. These coils can be made by winding some insulated copper wire on ordinary sewing thread spools, or even winding copper wire around tubes of some non-magnetic material.   Figure 33 shows two coils wound with No. 26 cotton covered wire on a sleeve of metal with round end pieces of fibre to hold the core together.   When you have connected these coils together and to a battery touch the ends in a pile of iron filings and you will get the results shown in Figure 33.

Figure 34 shows a pair of these coils with a horseshoe s h a p e d yoke placed through them.   If you make one of these devices you

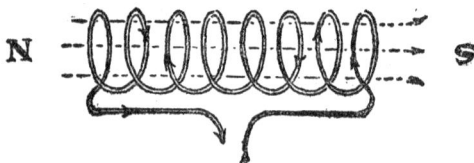

FIG. 32

must be careful and use soft iron for the yoke and also remember to connect the coils with the battery so that the lower end of one will produce a south pole and the other a north pole. This you can do by remembering the right hand rule given above in connection with Figure 32 so that you will have the current flowing in one direction in one coil and in the opposite way in the other. If you wind a coil of several layers such as is shown in the picture, connect the top wire of one coil to the bottom of the other and you will accomplish the required polarity.   After you have made this device try it out in the experiments where you have previously used the horseshoe or bar magnet and you will find that this is much stronger than either of the others and in addition, when the current is not flowing, this magnet loses its power.   Such a magnet is called an electro magnet.

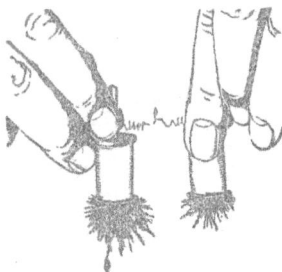

FIG. 33

FORCE IN THE EASIEST MAGNET PATH

Place iron filings on a glass plate and hold a horseshoe magnet under as shown in Figure 15.   The iron filings set themselves in lines showing the field of magnetism running from one pole to the other.   Place a small chip of iron or a piece of the soft iron wire between the poles of the magnet as in Figure 35 and you will notice

FIG. 34

that the iron filings crowd together directly over this, showing that magnetic lines find iron or steel the easiest path through which to travel and they crowd themselves into that path when possible.   For this reason the iron core in the coil of the electric magnet makes it much stronger than it would be if we depended upon the coil alone.

Boy Scouts should understand how to make an electro-magnet as explained above in order to pass their Boy Scout examination.

Now you have something which is used a great deal in various kinds of work and Figure 36 shows one of them.   This electro-magnet is used for unloading cars of heavy iron. In the picture, you will see several hundred pounds of pig iron clinging to the bars of the magnet.

The magnet is usually suspended on a crane or derrick so that it can be swung from one place to another and raised or lowered to do the lifting. First, it is lowered to the place where the iron is resting. The electricity is turned on and the big chunks

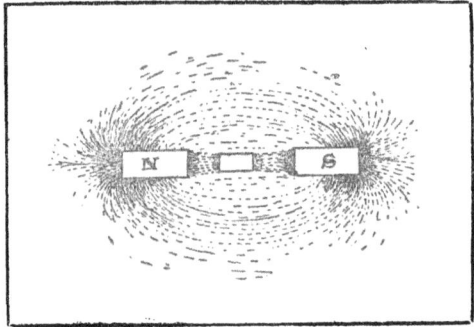

FIG. 35

of iron jump up and cling securely to the bottom of the magnet. Then the derrick is swung up in the air and around to the unloading point, the current turned off and the iron falls at once. The magnet is swung back over the iron and continues back and forth until the entire load has been moved. How much faster and better this is than the old fashioned way of having six or seven men load the pieces one by one on a box swung by an ordinary derrick and then having to unload them again.

You can make one of these magnetic loaders easily with your little electro-magnet and have lots of fun transferring iron wire, etc., from one spot to another.

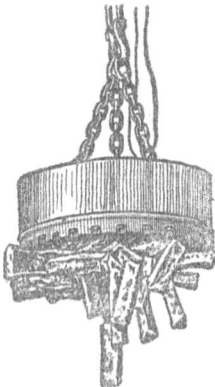

FIG. 36

MAGNET MOTOR

Now that we have found that a coil of wire is similar to a bar or horseshoe magnet when a current is flowing in it, we are ready to believe that a permanent magnet will act on an electro-magnet.

We can try this by suspending the electro-magnet in front of one pole of a bar magnet which has been laid on top of one of the corks. When the current is turned on, the coil will move according to the attraction or repulsion of the bar magnet. Now, if the current

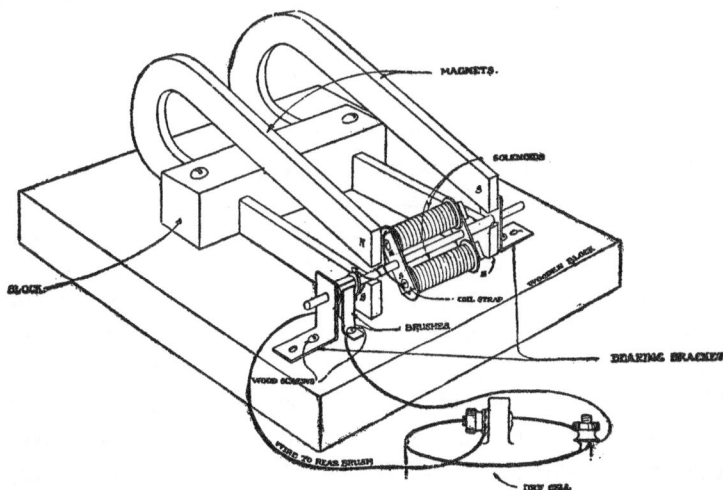

FIG. 37

is reversed, the coil will move in the opposite direction. If we are able to change the direction of the current fast enough, the coil will swing backward and forward like a pendulum. We can, by attaching a little rod to the core, turn a crank, producing a motor having the same action as the steam engine known as the reciprocating engine. A much better motor is shown in Figure 37.

This motor was made with two 6-inch horseshoe magnets and the description below covers a motor of this size. Should you have horseshoe magnets of a different size, you can readily make a similar motor by changing the proportions of the different parts. First, place two horseshoe magnets side by side as shown in the picture. Clamp them in place on a wooden block by means of a smaller wooden block, approximately 2½ inches long and 1 inch square on the ends. This block should be cut out so that it fits tightly over one side of each of the magnets. Be sure that when these magnets are in place one of them has its north pole upmost and the other with the north pole at the bottom. Next wind two little electro magnets or solenoids about 1 inch long. Those in the picture were made by first bending up a thin sheet of metal around a screw, slipping two round discs about ¾ inch diameter made of red fibre or heavy pasteboard over the ends of it. Between these discs lay over the tin about three wrappings of thin paper (writing paper will do), pasting in place. In order to make the fibre discs tight on the ends of the metal you can hammer the metal over, after the paper is in place, so that the ends are spread larger than the hole in the washers. Pierce two little holes in each washer with a small nail, one hole being as near the center and one as near outside as it is possible to make them. These are for the ends of the wire which is next to be wound on. Poke one wire through the center hole in one of the fibres and then wind as tightly as possible five or six layers of a wire about No. 24 or No. 26 Brown & Sharpe gauge. This may be either enamel covered or cotton covered. Two of these solenoid coils are required. Next make two strips of brass ⅜ inch wide and 1⅜ inches long, brass .040 inch thick is very good for this purpose. These pieces must have a hole through the center for the shaft and two holes at the end for the screws which will hold the coils in place. When these pieces are complete, put two screws, which you will use to bind the coils together, through the outside holes of one strip. Then set the coils on, so that when the current is sent through them, the end of one coil, under the head of the screw will be north, the opposite end of the other coil will be north. The text above will explain how to do this. On the other end of the coils place the second brass strip over the screws, then tighten both in place by two nuts. The screws used in the model made for Figure 37 were two steel round head machine screws, 6-32 thread, 1⅛ inches long. The shaft is made of brass rod approximately 3¾ inches long and ⅛ inch diameter. The bearing brackets for holding the shaft are made of brass .040 inch thick bent in an "L" shape, with holes for screwing them to the board and holes for the shaft to stick through at such a height that they will hold the shaft half way between the two poles of the magnet. Two brushes must be made also of an "L" shape. This can be made of .010 or .015 brass 3/16 inch wide, and when screwed to the board they must stand up at least ⅞ inch. The commutator or device for carrying the current through the brushes to the coils is the next thing and is the hardest to make. It is shown most clearly in Figure 38 and consists of two round fibre discs with holes through their center, so that they fit tightly on the shaft. Their outside diameter is about ½ inch. Then two pieces of brass .040 inch thick are formed in a rounded shape, with small ends make to stick through the fibre so that they fasten the two fibres and themselves together, leaving a space between each brass segment just dividing these so that they divide the circle which they form into two equal parts. A very convenient way to make these pieces would be to buy a piece of brass tubing and saw it in half. Also, instead of using fibre end pieces a small round block of wood could be made with a hole drilled through it, and the brass pieces could be fastened to the block by small pins. Great care must be used, however, if this method is followed, that the pins do not touch both brass pieces or rest against the shaft. The free ends of the magnet coils must be connected to the ends of the brass pieces on the commutator, as shown in Figure 38. Note that the break between the two brass pieces on the commutator is exactly on a horizontal line when the coils are directly one above the other.

B — 3

If you have placed your horseshoe magnets so that the north pole of one is at the bottom and the north pole of the other at the top and have made connections for your terminals as explained for the electro-magnet, your little motor will keep on turning until you shut off the current. How can we explain this action?

When the current is turned on, the ends of the steel screws become poles. Let us suppose that you have assembled your horseshoe magnet so its north pole stands in front of the electro-magnet's north pole. The other end of the magnet must be the south pole, and this stands in front of the horseshoe magnet's south pole. At the bottom polarities are reversed, but the same condition is found; that is, two like poles together. In our previous experiments, we found that like poles repel each other and that is true here. The north poles push against each other and the coil moves around, trying to get in front of the south pole, but when halfway around, the slot in the commutator causes the current to change its direction and the north pole changes to a south pole and tries to get away from the south pole of the permanent magnet, only to have the current reversed again; and so it keeps on jumping around and around the shaft, like poles being driven away from like poles and drawn toward unlike poles as long as the current flows.

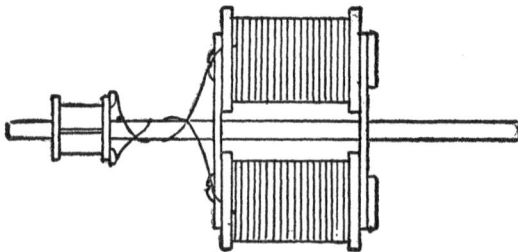

By using two or more dry batteries, or a current transformer, this little motor can be made to drive mechanical toys.

FIG. 38

Chapter III

ELECTRO-MAGNETIC INDUCTION

Now you may think we have reached the limit of electro-magnet investigation, for we can see how to build a motor, and our imagina-

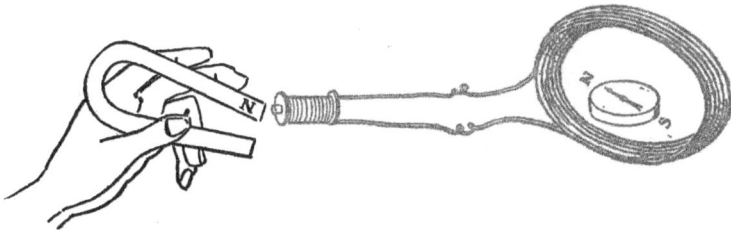

FIG. 39

tion readily pictures it running streets cars, elevators, machinery, etc., but there is one step further which was discovered by Faraday.

Make a solenoid coil and connect it to a coil of wire. The greater the number of turns of wire on the coil the better, unless the wire is very fine. Place the coil around the needle of a compass, as shown in Figure 39.

Now place the north pole of a permanent magnet in front of the solenoid and, remove it quickly. Place it back again. If you watch carefully, you see a slight movement of the needle. Faraday discovered this and formed the belief that, by moving the wire through the field of a permanent magnet or by moving the field so as to cut across the wire or other conductor, a flow of electric current is started by induction through the wire. He

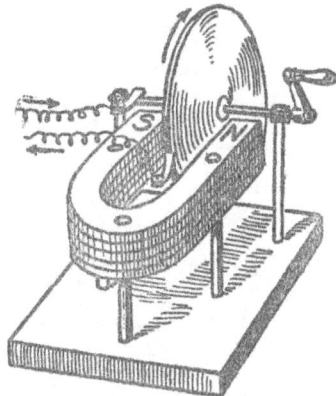

FIG. 40

finally made a machine, as shown in Figure 40, which you can easily copy with horseshoe magnets.

He placed a copper disc on a metal shaft between the poles of the horseshoe magnet. On an edge of the disc he placed a brush and another brush on the shaft, and connected wire to these. He revolved the handle so that the disc turned around in the direction of the arrow.   He found that the current flowed out of one wire into the other after they were joined.

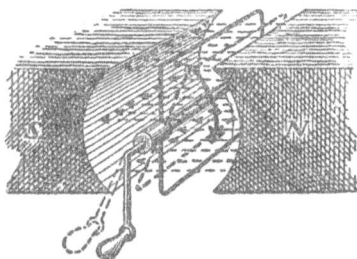

FIG. 41

Figure 41 shows the next step with a copper wire bent around the shaft in place of the copper disc. This gives the same result

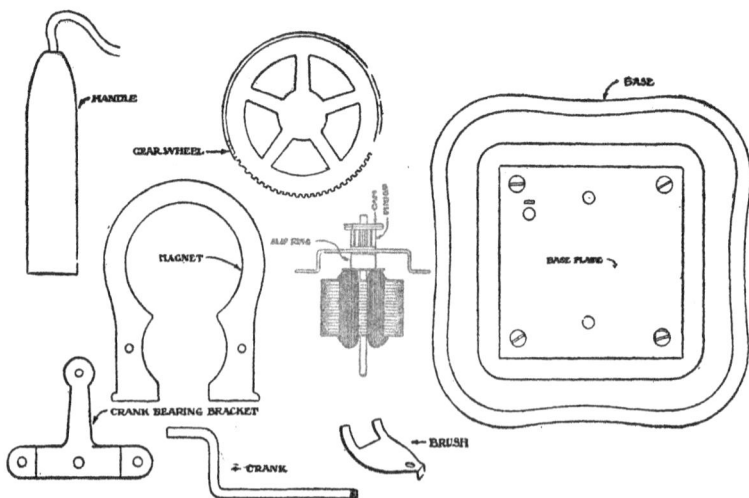

FIG. 42A

as before, with the exception that in one position no current flows. In the position 90° from this, the most current flows. Between these, the current rises from zero to the highest value, then falls again to zero. This is due to the fact that the wire conductor will cut none of the lines of magnetic force in one position, while in the other, it is cutting the greatest number. It is extremely hard to measure a current in one turn of wire such as shown in the picture, but we can increase the action by putting several turns of wire around the shaft.

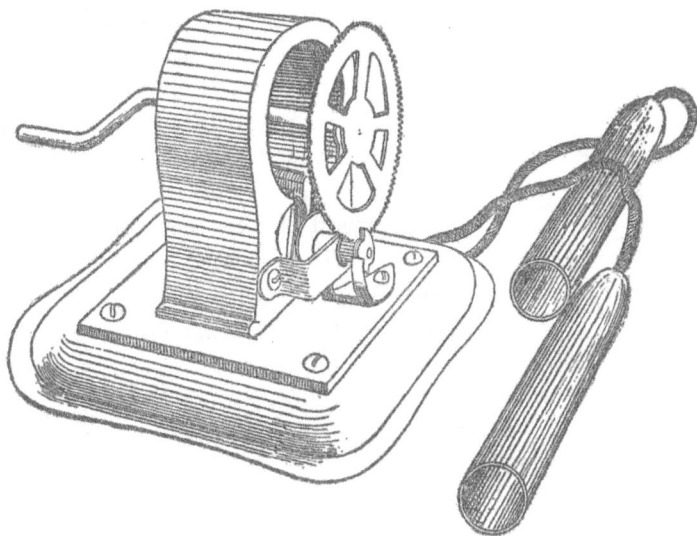

FIG. 42B

A device commonly known as a magneto or shocker illustrates this principle very well. You do not have to measure the electricity with a compass in this machine, for you can feel it by taking hold of the handles on the ends of the flexible copper cords when someone turns the crank which drives the armature around. Figure 42A shows the various parts of the magneto with their names.

Figure 42B shows the method of assembling this magneto. The strength of electricity increases in accordance with the speed in which the handle is turning the armature.

You can also make a little dynamo by changing the winding on one of these machines which can operate other motors and electric lights.

The motors described have used permanent magnets to produce a magnetic field. The earliest motors and generators were all made in this way. Later it was discovered even soft iron wire or soft iron plates retained a little magnetism, which is called residual magnetism. As stated in regard to the electro-magnet, the yoke or core made the magnetic lines produced by the coil of wire crowd themselves through it rather than pass through the air.

FIG. 43

Relying upon these peculiarities, motors and generators were then built which had coils of wire connected, so that, when current is flowing, they set up north and south poles which act on the revolving part, commonly called armature, just as the force from the permanent magnets acted on the armature between them. These are the types of motors and generators now commonly used.

The difference between a motor and a generator is that a motor is a machine which takes in electricity and gives out mechanical power. A generator is driven by mechanical power and gives out electric current. A generator depends upon the residual magnetism to start the electricity which flows into the winding, after which the field magnet coils are able to build up to the full amount for which the machine is designed. The motor does not require the residual magnetism as the coils receive the current from an outside source as soon as the circuit is closed.

In the experiments given above for electro-magnets, battery current was used. This current is continuous or direct, because it flows continuously in one direction. This gives a steady pull on the magnet.

There are also alternating and pulsating currents which are not steady but flow in surges like waves moving over the sea. Magnets and solenoids for alternating currents are not good for lifting because the magnetism pulsates due to the changing in electricity. They can be used for a number of things where this feature is not objectionable.

All alternating current motors, generators and transformers depend upon magnetism for their operation, but this magnetism is so closely connected with the study of alternating current that it cannot be properly described here in this short space. We can remember, however, that as the electric current changes in direction in a wire, flowing from zero to its highest value, then turning around in the other direction until it is at zero again, that, in strict accordance with the rules and experiments given above for magnetism around a wire, the magnetism revolves backward and forward around the wire and changes in strength following the changes in current.

MAGNETIC SATURATION

We have found that electro-magnets are much stronger than permanent magnets, but there is a limit to the amount of magnetic force a piece of iron or steel can contain, which is called "THE POINT OF SATURATION". The iron and steel seem to soak up magnetism just as a sponge soaks up water until it is thoroughly filled.

We have gone through the field of magnetism from the time of the earliest discoveries to the present. Although we do not know what magnetism is, we do know that other wonderful things seem to be related to it. One theory is that atoms are made up of electro-magnetic units called electrons. Light, magnetism and electricity appear to be much the same. Astronomers find that occurrences on the sun affect magnetic needles and that, undoubtedly, sun spots are caused by magnetism. Even gravitation is thought to be caused by some natural magnetic force which attracts all things toward the earth.

It is a mystery to be solved, and in studying it, some of us will discover new wonders for the use of our fellowmen just as Marconi, who astonished the world with his wireless telegraph.

To a real live boy, is not finding out these things far better than dreaming of enchanted castles, magic carpets and similar adventures?

Chapter IV

MAGNETIC TOYS AND TRICKS

MAGNETIC TIGHT ROPE WALKER

Cut some colored paper to represent the front of a stage and hang a horseshoe magnet behind it, so that it will be out of sight of the observers. Hang a stout thread across the stage.

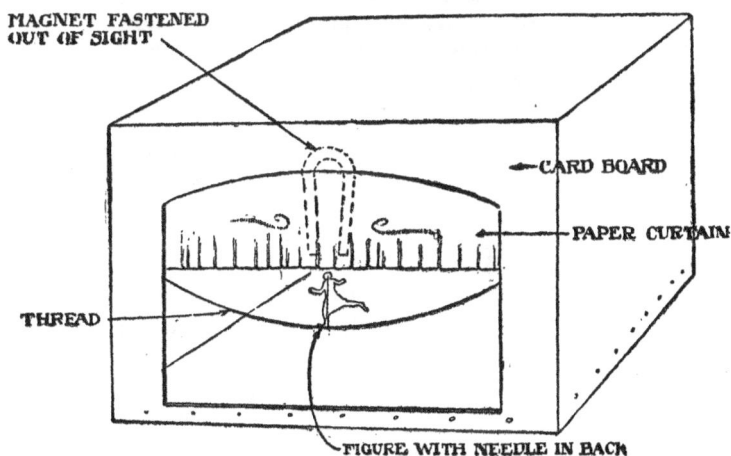

FIG. 44

Cut out little figures of tight-rope walkers from some stiff paper and fasten a steel needle on the back of them, as shown in the picture. Place the tight-rope walkers or acrobats on the thread so that the point of the needle sticks in the thread slightly. See Figure 44. Of course you must arrange this thread so that the head of the figures come directly under the magnet, but not too close, or the pull of the magnet will draw it up.

When the figures are arranged in the best position, they will stand up and sway just as tight-rope walkers balance themselves on the slack wire.

MAGIC PENCIL

Take an ordinary lead pencil and split the wood carefully in two pieces. Remove a portion of the lead, as in Figure 45. Magnetize a steel needle, about the same thickness as the lead, and insert in place of the lead. Stick the wood of the pencil together again, using glue

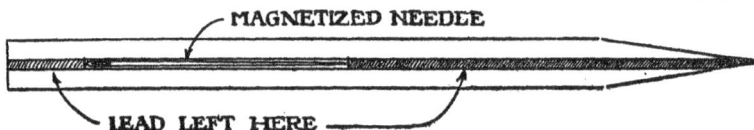

MAGNETIZED NEEDLE

LEAD LEFT HERE

FIG. 45

or shellac, and you have magic wand which will attract small iron and steel pieces to it and cause your compass needle to be attracted or repelled at will.

MAGNETIC NAVY

Make some small wood boats, such as shown in Figure 46, using paper for the sails. Drive a small nail, or, better still, a good-sized needle through the length of the wood.

NEEDLE OR STEEL WIRE IN THE WOOD OR FASTENED UNDERNEATH

BATH TUB OR LARGE BOWL

FIG. 46

By holding your magic pencil or your bar magnet toward these boats, they will sail around a dish of water or the bath tub in a most lifelike manner.

MAGNETIC JACK STRAWS

You can have a lot of fun playing Jack Straws in a new way by using pieces of soft iron wire. It will add to the fun to cut pieces

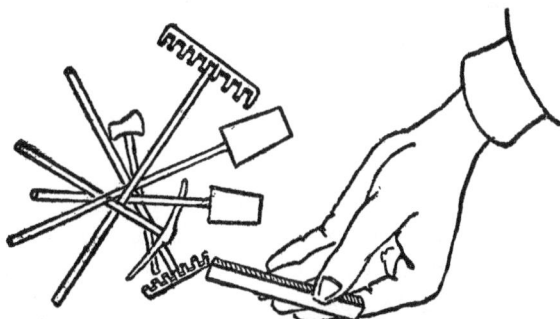

FIG. 47

of wood cork to stick on the ends of the wires, or you can mold forms with sealing wax with the wires and make little hammers, hoes, rakes or other articles, as in Figure 47. The game is played by two people in the same way that the old-fashioned game of Jack Straws is played. First drop the tools in a mixed pile. Each player is given a bar magnet and in turn tries to lift the tools out from the

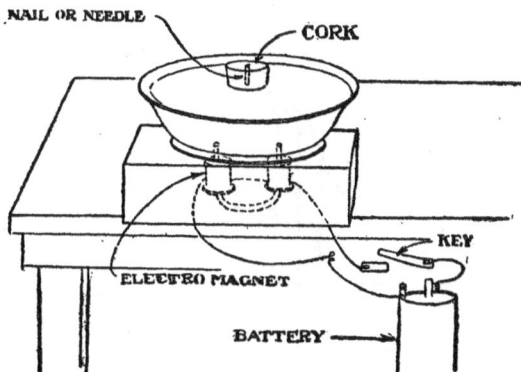

FIG. 48

pile one at a time. The player continues to lift them from the pile until he drops one. He then loses his turn and the other player begins. The game continues until all the articles are removed from the pile and the player having the largest number is declared the winner. This game can be varied by giving numbers to each article. These numbers are added at the end of the game and the player having the highest total is the winner.

MAGIC CORK

Conceal a large nail or needle in a cork and place in a shallow dish of water under which you have hidden an electro-magnet Figure 48. Connect the wires of the electro-magnet to a battery and make a key, using two pieces of flat brass or copper. Arrange this under a table so that you can press it with your foot. Now tell your friends that you can make the cork sink or swim at your command. If you can fix a head and arms on the cork to resemble a diver, this trick will be much more amusing. When you want him to go down, close the electric circuit and the magnet will pull the needle in the man toward the bottom of the dish, it will bob up again when the circuit is opened.

FIG. 49

Another way to make this trick work would be to cut a pasteboard jumping jack, as shown in Figure 49. The string moving the arms and legs should be fastened to the solenoid coil. Closing the circuit makes the little man dance and wave his arms.

MAGNETIC VIBRATION RECORDER

Stick a magnetized needle upright in a cork and beside it place a soft iron wire, with the upper end bent as shown in Figure 50. Magnetize another needle and let it hang by attraction to the iron wire directly over the first needle so that the like poles are together. This device placed on a table or desk will record the slightest vibration in the room and will continue to swing for some time.

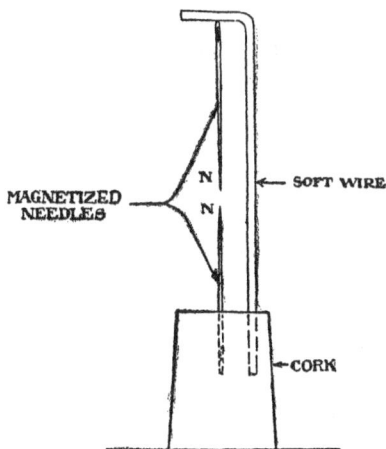

FIG. 50

MAGNETIC TOP

Magnetize a large steel darning needle. Cut a round disc of cardboard and stick the needle through the center, making a top which you can spin with your fingers. See Figure 51. Bend some soft iron pieces in shapes like snakes or s's. Set your top spinning as near one of these as possible and the top will travel along around in front and back of the wire in a most peculiar manner.

SLIDING TRICK

Take a long heavy piece of cardboard and fasten over a board at an incline with a space between so that your horseshoe magnet can slide in it. See Figure 52. Tie a stout black thread to the magnet so you can raise or lower it. Place a disc of iron, or some other piece of iron or steel, at the bottom of the cardboard toboggan slide

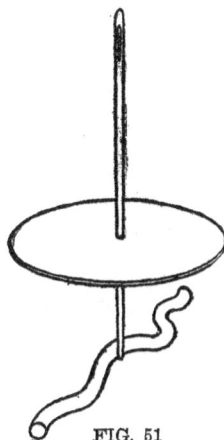

FIG. 51

and lower the magnet until it is directly under the steel piece. Then, as you pull the magnet, the steel will be drawn up the incline.

MAGNETS IN TELEPHONES

Some of the smallest electro-magnets are used in telephones. When you talk into a telephone transmitter your voice sends waves of air against the transmitter diaphragm (B-Figure 53). The diaphragm then vibrates from each wave stroke and in doing so compresses or releases the grains of carbon in the little cup directly in

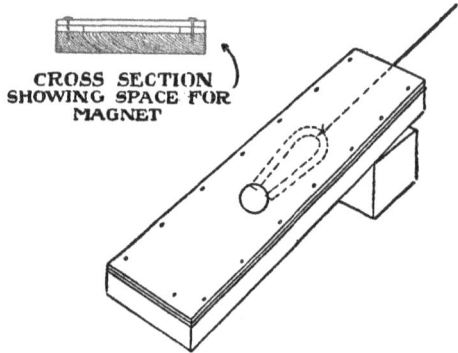

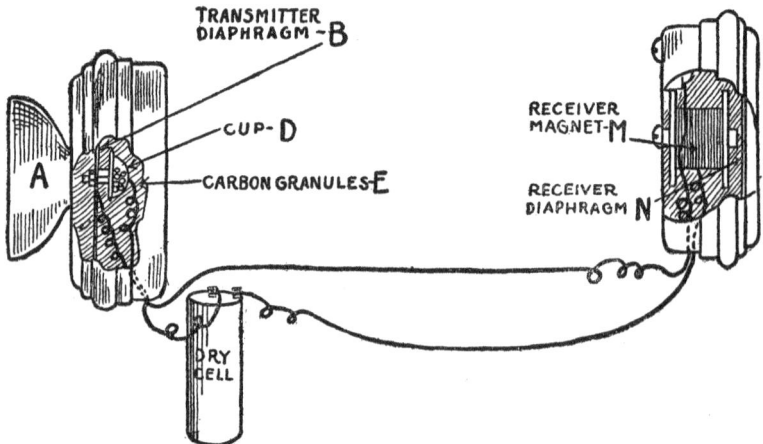

CROSS SECTION
SHOWING SPACE FOR
MAGNET

FIG. 52

TRANSMITTER
DIAPHRAGM - B

CUP - D

CARBON GRANULES - E

A

RECEIVER
MAGNET - M

RECEIVER
DIAPHRAGM N

DRY
CELL

FIG. 53

the rear. This sets up a changing resistance in the circuit in which is the receiver. The receiver consists mainly of an electro-magnet in front of which is a thin disc of magnetic material.

, As there is a current flowing in the phone circuit, the change of resistance caused by the action of the tones of the speaker's voice on the transmitter causes the current in the electro-magnet in the receiver to vary with each change in resistance. The change makes the electro-mag-net change its strength, t h u s rapidly varying its pull on the magnetic d i s c in front of it. And these vi-brations being a true copy of the v i b r a t ions of the voice speak-ing i n t o t h e transmitter give to the ear of the listener a copy o f a l l t h e sounds from the person speaking.

FIG. 54

WIRELESS PUP

A very amusing toy has been made which uses a small electro-magnet, and also works somewhat on the principle of the telephone. This is illustrated in Figure 54.   The parts are simple and you can easily make one to amuse and astonish your friends.

At the five and ten-cent store you can buy a little toy dog, or, if

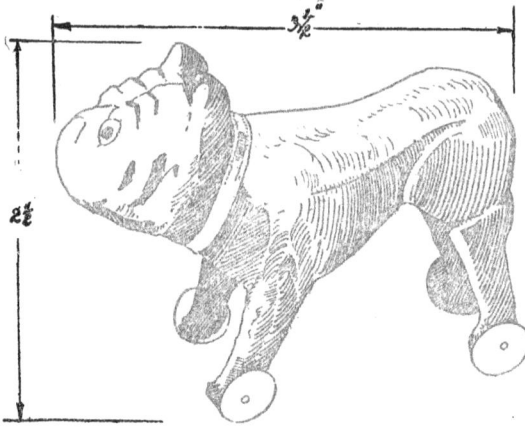

Back
FIG. 54A

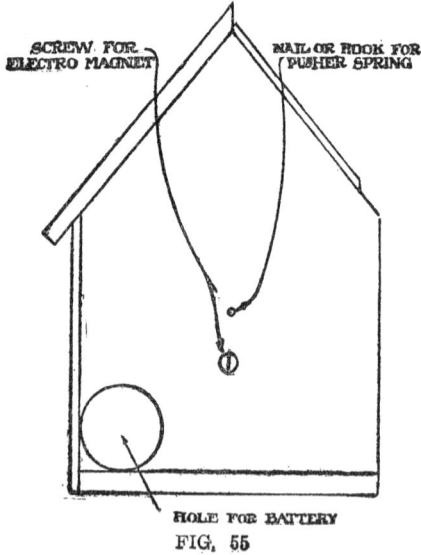

SCREW FOR
ELECTRO MAGNET

NAIL OR HOOK FOR
PUSHER SPRING

HOLE FOR BATTERY
FIG. 55

you prefer, whittle one out of wood, and by means of small nails or pins fasten little wheels made of tin to each foot. Make the pup as light as possible and about as large as shown in Figure 54A.

The dog house is next. This is best made from thin wood, though heavy cardboard will serve the purpose very well. See Figures 54 and 56.

Front same as back except for door, as shown in Figure 55.

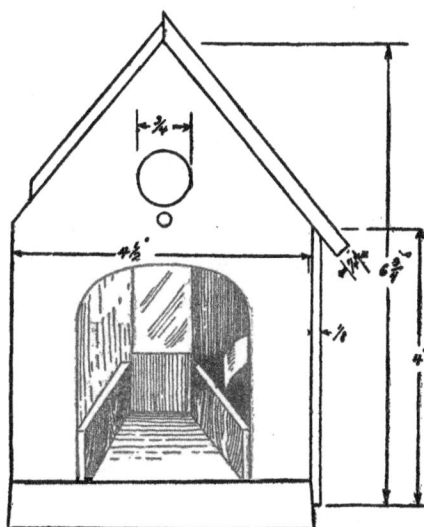

FIG. 56

The operation of this device depends on two properties: first, the action of sound waves against a swinging contact breaker; second, the action of the pull of an electro-magnet. The electric circuit contains a small metal disc, aluminum, brass or iron, suspended in back of the circular opening in the house front. This disc rests very lightly against the smooth head of a brass or nickel-plated screw. From the screw a wire is carried to one side of a small flash-light battery, and if you buy the small round batteries as shown in the picture remember that the outside of the battery is one contact—the small brass knob at the end is the other. Connect the other side of the battery to the electro-magnet. The second lead of the magnet is connected to the screw on which the diaphragm is hung. See Figures 57A, B and C for connections.

The outfit is now ready for use. Place it on a level place, such as a shelf or table. Push the dog into the house, facing the door.

B — 4

He will strike the pusher and force it back against the end of the electro-magnet core, at the same time closing the electric circuit. This sends a current through the coils of the magnet and causes the core of the magnet to grip the pusher and hold it.

Now stand a few feet in front of the house and whistle, clap your hands or call sharply to the pup. The vibrations of the air caused by your voice will make the disc sway slightly, causing a momentary open circuit. This destroys the magnetism holding the pusher back, and the spiral spring will then make the pusher shove the dog out in a hurry.

In making such a toy too much care cannot be taken in adjusting the disc so that it will swing freely, and, also, in keeping the various contacts clean and bright.

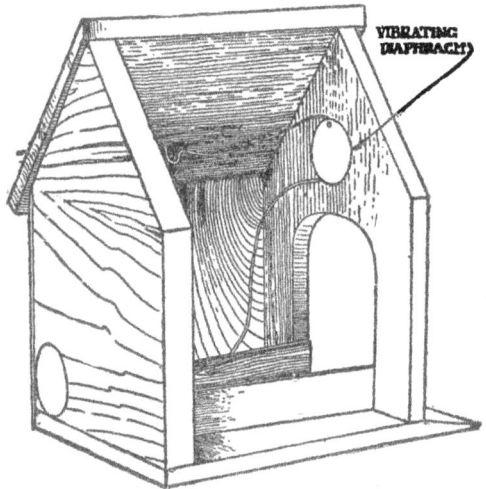

FIG. 57A

A CIRCUIT BREAKER

In the electric power houses and other places where a large amount of current is flowing, circuit breakers are used in order to save fuses. These have electro-magnets so arranged that when the current gets too strong the magnetism pulls a plunger which is attached to a switch. This switch then opens the circuit, stopping the overflow of current. Some of these are also arranged so that they break the circuit if the pressure (voltage) gets dangerously high.

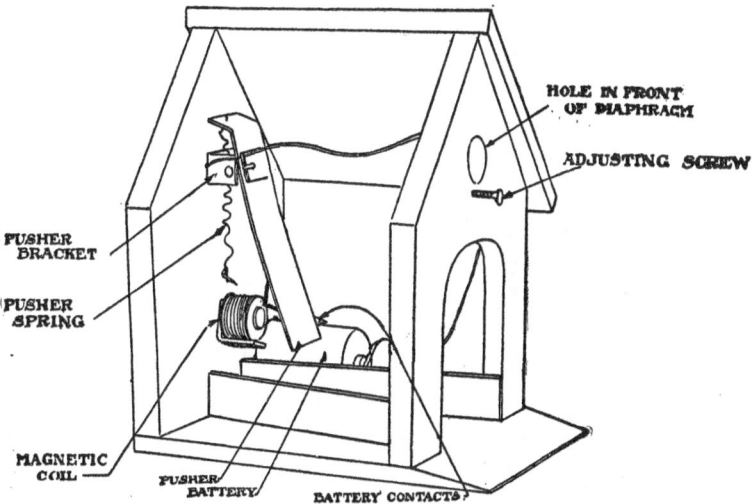

FIG. 57B

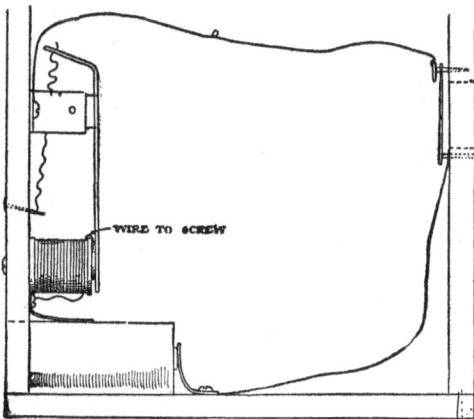

FIG. 57C

Still another kind is used where storage batteries are charged. These work backward from the other two described; that is, the magnets hold the plunger up and keep the circuit switch closed until the current (or voltage) goes down too low. When the current drops, open goes the switch, because the magnetism no longer pulls against the spring.

A simple circuit breaker can be made with a coil of wire wound of No. 24 Brown & Sharpe gauge copper (insulated) wire wound in spool form. If you have an old empty spool wind it full of wire. Have a round piece of soft iron wire in it.

The soft iron wire should have a hole drilled in it near the upper end and a small brass spring fastened through the hole.

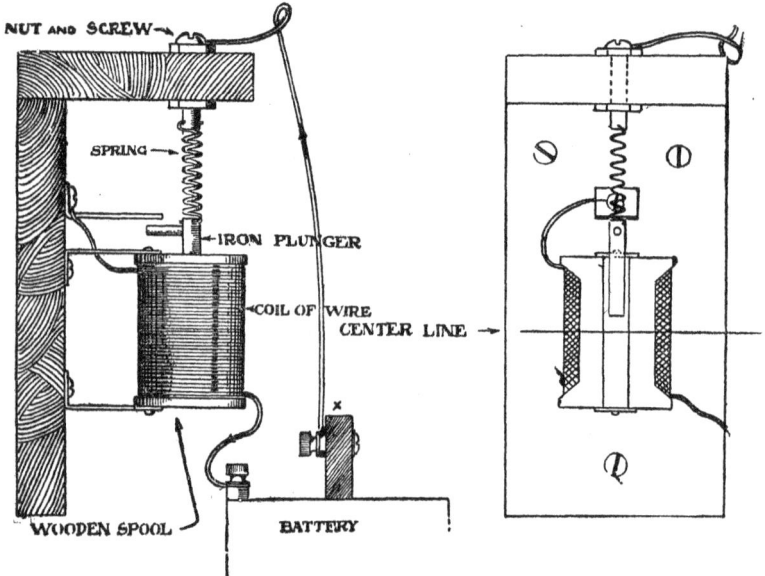

FIG. 58

The upper end of the spring is fastened in a hole in machine screw, as shown in Figure 58. The screw is locked in place in a wooden block mounted on the top of the base. Fasten one wire from the battery to the screw and the other side of the battery to one wire on the coil. The remaining wire from the coil is carried to a pin on the base board. This pin is in such a position that the lower end of the spring, which is brought through the plunger, closes the circuit when the spring is supporting the plunger at rest. As the current flows, the plunger is drawn down into the center of the coil and then the circuit is broken at the pin. This allows the magnetism to die out and the spring then pulls the plunger back into position. This model shows the working principles of the real circuit b r e a k e r s, though of course they are much more

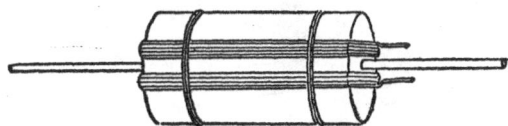

FIG. 59

elaborate. The type of electro-magnet just described is called the plunger type, due to the fact that it tries to suck the moving plunger into its center hole. Do not use a solenoid which has a steel sleeve around its center hole. This causes the plunger to stick to it rather than permitting it to be drawn inside. Plunger magnet coils give the strongest pull at the center of the coil.

SMALL MOTOR

A small motor can be made which will further prove the theories shown by previous experiments, though the motor will give very little power.

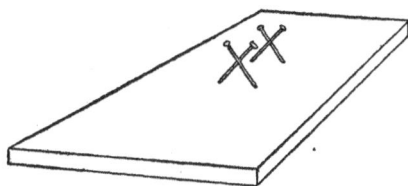

FIG. 60

Take a cork or round piece of soft wood about ¾ inches in diameter and from an inch to 1½ inches long. Stick a long wire or a needle through the center of this cylinder just as near the center as possible, so that the armature will be in balance. Next wind on the spool about 100 turns of fine copper wire, putting 50 turns each side of the shaft.

Bring the start and finish of the winding out at one end, parallel to the shaft, and cut them off so they stand off about ¼ inch. Bind the winding in place with a few turns of thread, as in Figure 59.

Drive four small nails into a block of wood, as shown in Figure 60, for bearing.

Place two bar magnets on blocks so that the "N" pole of one and

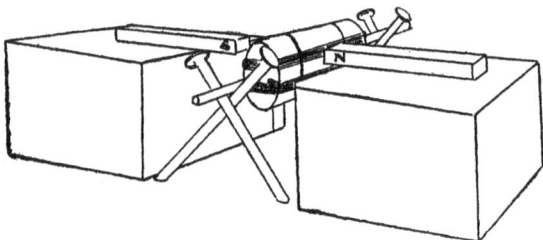

FIG. 61

the south pole of the other are opposite the armature.

Lay the armature in place on the bearings, as in Figure 61. Now connect a pair of stout wires to a dry battery and clean the opposite ends.

Hold these ends in one hand, lightly touching the tips of the armature, and with your free hand give the armature a little spin. It will go in one direction only, so you may have to spin it again in the opposite direction from what you did at first, but you will find one direction in which it will revolve quite rapidly. Of course this is a weak little thing, so you must be careful not to press the wires from the battery too hard on the armature. If you do, it will prevent the motor from running. If you happen to have a horseshoe magnet, as in Figure 62, with the

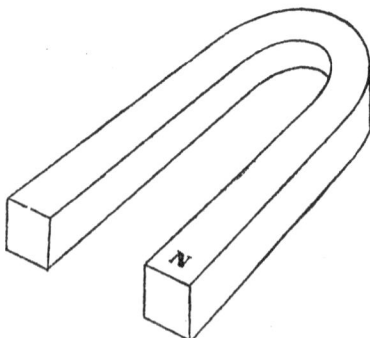

FIG. 62

poles far enough apart you can use this in place of the bar magnets.

MAGNETIC GUN

Make a solenoid coil by winding several layers of No. 26 Brown & Sharpe gauge insulated wire around a paper or brass tube. Make the tube ¼ inch in diameter. Build up the winding about as shown in the picture. Put a small round-headed screw in the center hole and place the coil in a tilted position, as shown in Figure 63. Place

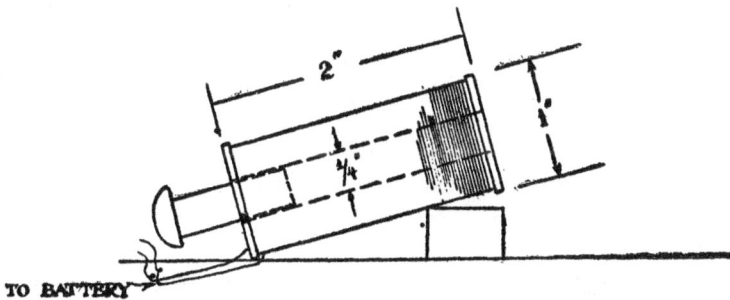

TO BATTERY

FIG. 63

little cork balls or some other light material in the cannon in front of the screw. Connect the wires from the coil to three or four dry cells and the screw will be quickly pulled into the hole, shooting the little bullet out. Be sure that the screw is less than 1 inch long. If you do not, the gun will not have the necessary force to be of any value.

A REGISTERING WIND VANE

Sometimes it would be very convenient if you didn't have to go where you could look at the weather vane to tell just how the wind is blowing. Make a vane of sheet steel, or brass, similar to that shown in Figure 64. Fasten a "U" shaped brass strip securely to the metal vane.

Next make a circular block of wood about 5 inches in diameter and 1 inch thick. Drill a hole through its center for the supporting shaft of the wind vane. Now screw some flat strips of brass around the top of the block, as shown in Figure 65.

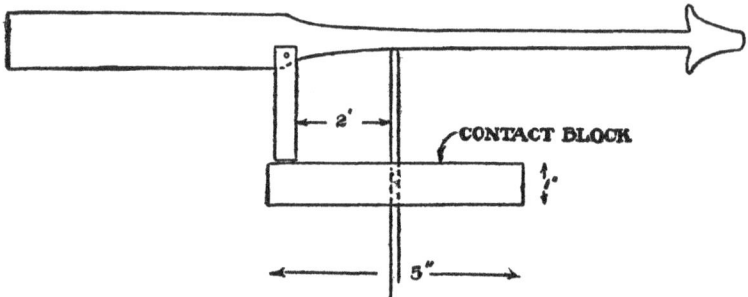

FIG. 64

The four single strips should be spaced around the circle for the North, East, South and West positions. The narrow strips should be placed halfway between the others so that when the brass contact on the vane swings over them it will rest on each one. Connect the

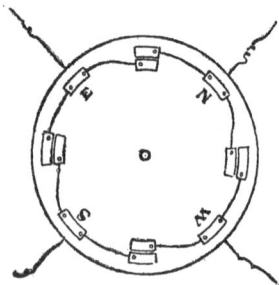

FIG. 65

narrow strips to the broad ones as shown in the figure. The best way to do this will be to drill holes in the wood and pushing brass or copper wire through and solder the ends to the strips. Place this contact board in position under the weather vane so that the brass strip on the vane will rub on the brass strips of the block as it turns around.

In order to set the board in the proper position, it will be necessary to know just what time noon, by *sun time,* is; this may be several minutes before or after your clock time. But while you are working on the apparatus you can write to the nearest Government weather bureau and learn just what time, sun time noon, at your home is. After you have found just when this is, you will find that at that moment shadows of any vertical body point directly north. By locating the shadow on the shaft of the weather vane at this instant, you will be able to set the North

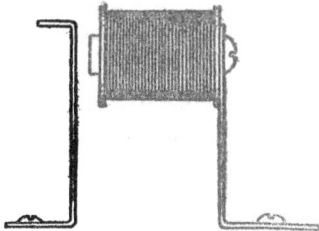

FIG. 66A

and South points of your block in line with this shadow. After setting the block in the true position fasten it securely in place, taking care that it is level and that the contact point on the vane touches all the eight points on the block. Next fasten insulated copper wires to each of the North, South, East and West points on the board, also one on the shaft of the weather vane, and carry the other ends of the wire down to the place where you want the

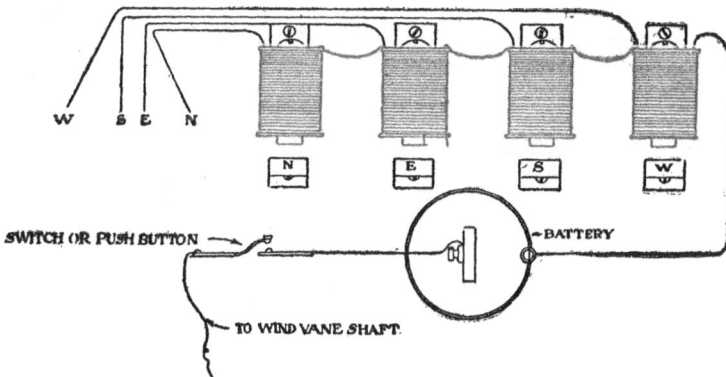

FIG. 66B

under-tug device to be placed. It will save a great deal of trouble if you put a tag or mark of some kind on each wire so you may know to which contact it is connected. A very simple indicator can be made of four coils.

Wind these coils of insulated wire (No. 24 to 28). A coil ¾ inches long with a 3/16 inch hole through it, and the outside of the winding built up to ⅝ inch diameter will serve the purpose very nicely, like Figure 66A. Put a steel screw through each coil and fasten the coils in a row on a board, as shown in Figure 66B. Under each coil mount a piece of soft iron or steel ⅜ inch wide and shaped like that in Figure 66A.

Complete the electrical circuit, as shown in the picture, using two or three dry batteries and a switch or door bell push button. On

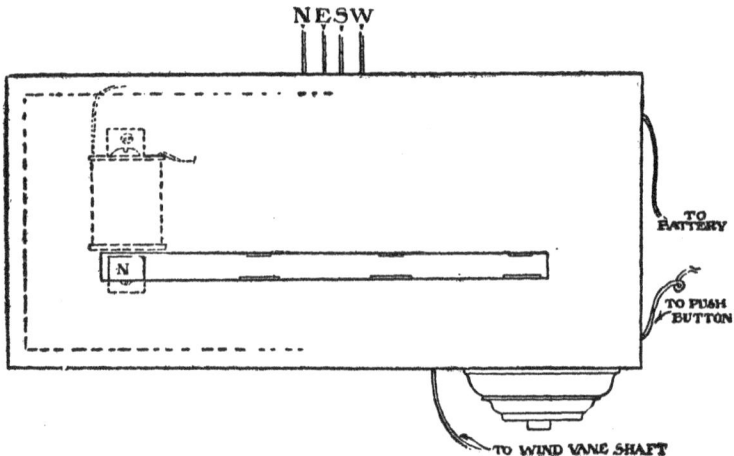

FIG. 67

the end of the arms you can paste the letters "N", "E", "S", and "W", which can be cut from any magazine or newspaper advertisement.

This device will work as follows: If the wind points the vane to the West, the contact on the vane will be touching the flat contact on the block, and if the switch is then closed, the magnet in that circuit will pull the steel arm under it up to the end of the steel screw. If the wind is blowing half way between North and West

(North West), the moving contact will be touching the two small flat plates, one in the "N" circuit and one in the "W" circuit; and closing the switch at that instant will make the "N" and "W" steel indicators jump up to the ends of the magnet cores. If the indicators show a tendency to stick to the screw heads, paste a piece of paper over the end of the screw, so the indicators cannot quite touch the cores.

It will keep the set in a much better condition if you put a little box with a glass front in it, as shown in Figure 67.

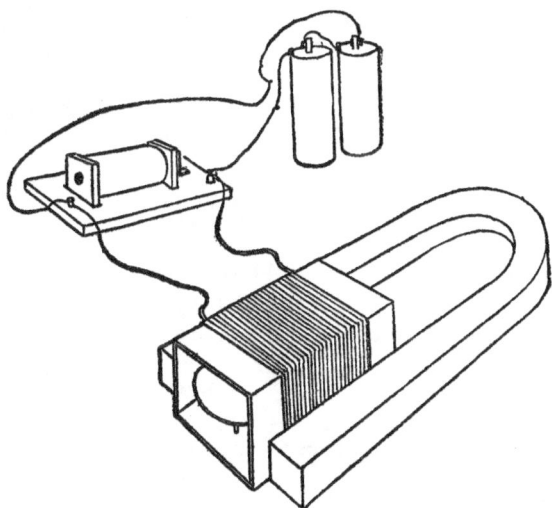

FIG. 68

ROTATING DISC

This experiment requires a magnet of the shape given in Figure 68 and a vibrating circuit breaker like that used on an induction coil.

Wind about one hundred feet of No. 28 cotton covered wire on a small form. The cover of a safety match box will serve very nicely. Figure 70.

Another piece required is a thin iron or steel disc about the size given in Figure 69.

Suspend this disc on a needle point by punching a little dent in the center of it. Put the coil of wire between the poles of the magnet and the disc inside the coil and on the needle point. Make sure the disc will turn freely. Connect the ends of the coil to the posts of the vibrator and also connect these posts to two or three dry batteries. When the circuit is complete, the disc will revolve rapidly.

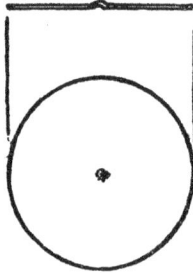

FIG. 69

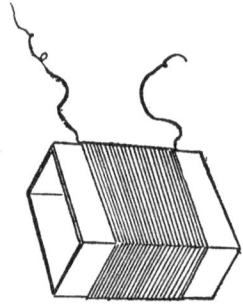

FIG. 70

INDUCTION COIL

Although the induction coil is much more than a magnetic toy, still it depends entirely on the electro-magnetic action for its make and break action, which controls the entire action of the apparatus.

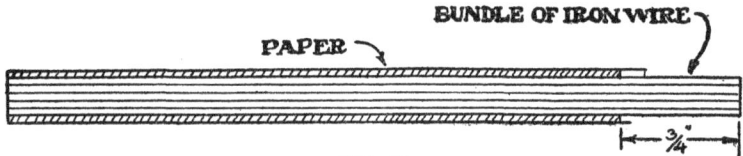

BUNDLE OF IRON WIRE

PAPER

FIG. 71

An induction coil, similar to Figure 71, can be easily made and will prove very useful to the experimenter in wireless or high voltage work of any kind.

THE CORE

The core is to be made of soft iron wire. (All alternating current magnets use small iron wire, while direct current cores are made of a solid piece. A solid bar would heat badly in an alternating current coil.) Get some stove pipe wire, size about .045 inches No. 17 Brown & Sharpe gauge. Cut 25 or 30 lengths of this wire 4¾ inches long. Make sure that these are straight. Wrap a bundle of these wires in four or five layers of paper, the thickness of ordinary writing paper. Paste the end of the paper down so that the wires will be held securely in place. The diameter of iron bundle should be about ¼ inch.

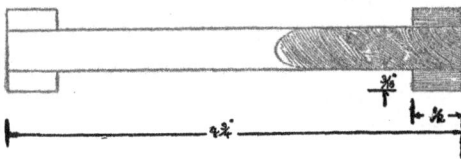

FIG. 72

Next take a round stick of wood the same length as the iron core and at least 1/16 inch larger than the outside of the paper. Wrap the ends of this stick with a paper strip ½ inch wide and glue it securely in place. It must build up the ends at least 3/16 inch. See Figure 72.

Lay two strings or threads along the stick, the strings each at least three times as long as the stick, fastening the ends around pins. See Figure 73.

Next carefully wind in even layers three layers of single cotton and enamel wire, size No. 18 Brown & Sharpe gauge (.0403), leaving about 18 inches sticking out from each end. When the winding is done, tie the string ends together over the top of the coil. Over the top of the wire wind three layers of stout paper, just about ⅛ inch longer than the coil. In order to do this you must remove the paper ends on your stick, but this can be done now that you have tied the string in place.

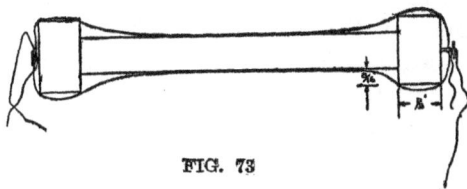

FIG. 73

Glue the paper securely in place. Now cut some cardboard or even thin board pieces 1 inch square, and put a hole in the center of these, so they will slip over the stick. See Figure 74.

Lock them in place by driving a nail through the end of the stick, or by building some paper ends up again as before. Lay two strings on again and wind on top of the paper some No. 36 silk and enamel insulated wire, building up this at least 3/8 of an inch. Six ounces of this wire will be plenty for this. Bring the ends of the string up and tie the coil securely in place. Now, you can remove the ends from the wooden block and knock the block out from the center.

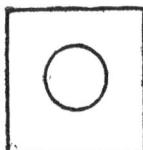

FIG. 74

Make two blocks of wood ½ inch thick, with a hole in the center large enough to stick the bundle of iron wire through and a small hole as near as possible to this larger one big enough to slip the end of the large wire (No. 18) through. See Figure 75. The block of wood must be big enough to project ⅛ of an inch beyond the outside of the wire coils. Slip the iron core inside the windings and then put the ends of the large wire through the small holes in the wooden blocks, and finally put the blocks over the ends of the iron wire. Screw these blocks to a board so they will fit snugly against the winding. See Figure 76.

Next fasten a piece of soft iron to a piece of spring brass, as shown in Figure 77.

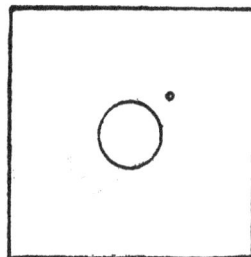

FIG. 75

The iron should be about ¼ inch in diameter and ⅛ inch thick. Fasten to the brass by soldering or by a flat-headed screw, but be sure the outside end of the iron is smooth and bright. The brass spring should be about 1/64 of an inch thick and bent in an "L" shape, so that when mounted in place the iron will be directly in front of and about ⅛ of an inch from the end of the iron wire.

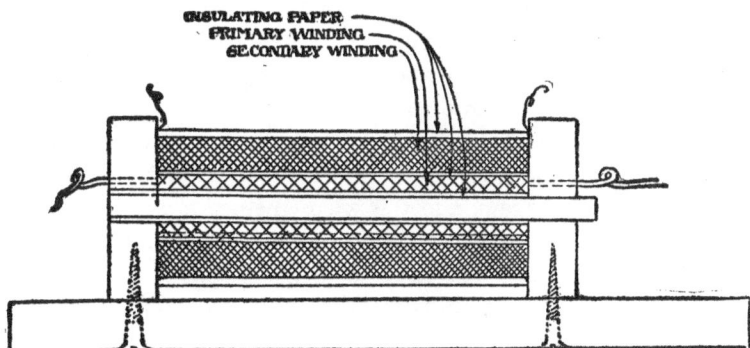

FIG. 76

Screw it to the base, as shown in Figure 78. Back of the spring put a wooden post and through it a brass machine screw with some locking nuts. This is the adjusting screw. At the top of the wooden blocks put a brass wood screw and a washer (you can cut this out of brass sheet) and connect the ends of the top winding to these screws.

CONNECTIONS

Connect one end of the primary winding, that is the large wire (No. 18), under the head of one of the screws holding the brass spring. Connect the other end of the same winding to a series of at least two dry batteries. (More batteries will give more power.)

Connect from the other side of the battery to the brass adjusting screw. The wires leading to the apparatus to which you want to supply the high voltage should be connected to the secondary binding screw (to which the small wire is fastened).

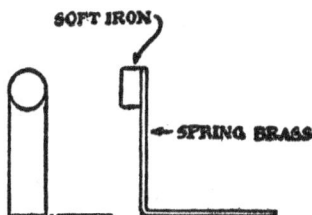

FIG. 77

OPERATION

When the circuit is complete, adjust the brass screw until the vibrator (the iron mounted on the brass spring) will bound back and forth rapidly. It will do this because the large wire magnetizes the bundle of iron wire which draws to it the small iron piece. But in drawing the iron away from the brass screw it breaks the electric current flow and the spring then flies back in position of rest only to close the circuit again, and this keeps the action going.

As explained previously, the current makes a magnetic field around the large wire. The strength of this magnetic field is determined by the number of turns of wire, and also by the amount of

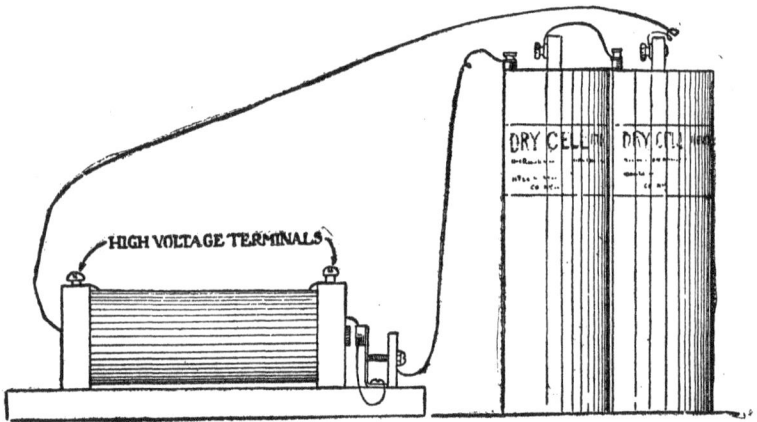

FIG. 78

current flowing. The current is changing from zero to its full value every time the vibrating arm makes and breaks the circuit. The magnetism must therefore change from zero to the high point for every current change. These changing lines of magnetism cut across the many turns of the fine wire on the secondary. It is well known that currents of electricity can be induced in a wire by moving the wire through a magnetic field so that it cuts the magnetic lines. AND THE SAME RESULT CAN BE GAINED IF THE WIRE IS STATIONARY, BUT THE MAGNETIC LINES MOVE SO THEY CUT ACROSS THE WIRE. In both cases the number of magnetic lines cut by the wire determines the voltage of the circuit. If the wire is coiled so as to form a long piece, it will cut or be cut by more magnetism than one short piece. Therefore, when the primary winding of the induction coil sets a varying magnetic field surging across the many

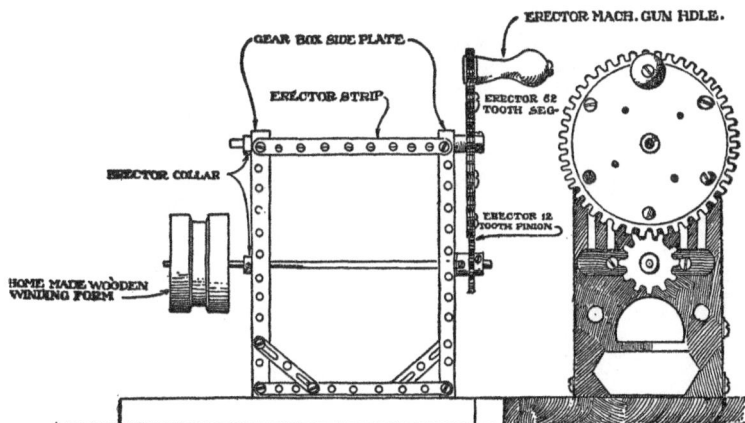

FIG. 79

turns of the secondary winding, it induces electrical flow at a higher voltage in the fine wires, and this can be taken off from the terminal posts. Caution must be observed in using such a device, for a severe shock can be received from the secondary of this machine when it is operating. Keep the hands away from the binding posts while it is working.

Figure 79 shows a simple winding machine made of construction toy parts which will be a great help in winding coils for such devices as this.

B — 5

IS THE ELECTRICITY IN YOUR HOUSE ALTERNATING OR DIRECT CURRENT?

Place one of your horseshoe magnets or your electro-magnets near the glass of any lighted incandescent lamp. If you will look carefully you will see that it sets up a disturbance of the glowing filament. If there is a direct current flowing in the lamp, the filament will be bent over by magnetic attraction or repulsion. If alternating current is flowing, you will see a decided vibration of the lighted filament.

MAGNETIC DESIGNS

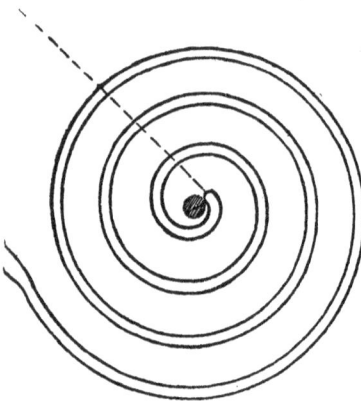

FIG. 80

BIFILAR WOUND COIL — DOTTED LINE SHOWS TAP AT MIDDLE POINT OF THE MAIN WIRE

Place several sewing needles through corks; magnetize them. Place the corks in a bowl of water. If you have placed them in the water with the ends of the same polarity sticking up and have pointed the north or the south pole of a bar magnet toward them, you will find that they group themselves into peculiar figures. After you have done this turn some of the needles upside down, some with the north poles and some with the south poles up. By approaching them with a bar magnet you will see some of them attracted and some repelled.

THE   FAKE   ELECT J-MAGNET

This is a stunt with which you can fool your friends, using what is known as the Bifilar winding, a picture of which is shown, Figure 80. Wind a coil with any number of turns of insulated wire, doubling the wire back on itself. Remember your right hand rule for current flowing through the wire. You will find that one-half of the winding will oppose the magnetism of the other half and that no magnetic effect will be produced by the coil. By placing the tap on the wire as shown in Figure 80, so that one-half of the coil can be cut from the current carrying circuit, you can produce magnetism. Arrange this tap so that it is well concealed and you have a coil by which you can produce magnetism when your friends cannot, much to their astonishment and your own enjoyment.

HANGING A RING OR KEY ON A PICTURE

A very amusing and astonishing trick can be done with the following apparatus: Behind a thin blackboard, a piece of drawing paper or some other material on which you can draw a picture, hang a strong electro-magnet, being careful to conceal it from the front of the board. Be sure that you know exactly where it is located. Now, tell your friends that you are able to draw a picture of a hook or nail so true to life that you can hang a key or steel ring or any other steel or iron piece on it. Draw a picture, then place the key or ring against the board. The magnet, of course, will hold the key in place.

MAGNETIC FINGERS

Conceal a piece of magnetized steel, the point of a sewing needle will work very well, under the finger nail of your first finger. By pointing your finger to a very small piece of iron or steel, you can attract it. The compass needle will turn around at your command.

MAGNETIC SEPARATORS

The fact that some materials are attracted by magnets and some are not have been used many years by manufacturers to separate the steel and iron filings and chips from brass, dust, etc. If you mix iron filings with dust and then hold a magnet over them, you will draw out the iron filings while the dirt particles will remain behind. One of the types of machines used by manufacturers is built as follows: An endless belt revolves over pulleys which carries the mixture to be separated downward to a magnet at the lower end of the belt. The material falls downward near the poles of a strong magnet and, as it falls, the steel or iron is pulled toward the poles, while the non-magnetic material falls in a straight line. A partition is set up, so that one pile of non-magnetic material accumulates on one side of it and on the other side of it iron or steel.

TO TELL IRON FROM BRASS

A great many pieces of furniture and ornaments are made of imitation brass. The material used is most often sheet iron plated and lacquered. You can prove whether it is real brass or imitation by attracting it with a magnet. If it is imitation, the material will, of course, stick to the magnet; whereas, with real brass the magnet will have no effect. You will also find that by attracting tin cans and other articles, made of so-called tin sheet, that these are not really made of tin, but of sheet iron with a thin plating of tin over them.

A TEST FOR LIVE WIRES

At some time or other, you may wish to know whether electric wires are carrying a current or whether there is any electricity in them. This is commonly known as finding out whether or not the conductors are live or dead. By bringing a compass near the wires or by suspending a magnetized needle near them, you will see the needle quiver if an alternating current is flowing in the wire. In case of direct current, you will have a decided deflection. If wires are of high voltage, such as found in power houses or on the so-called high tension lines, there is great danger of receiving a shock on these circuits. Only experienced electrical men should have anything to do with them.

ELECTRICAL PENDULUMS

Electrical clocks have been made which are controlled by a pendulum. This pendulum is kept in motion by an electro-magnet. To illustrate how this can be done place a coil of wire with a screw

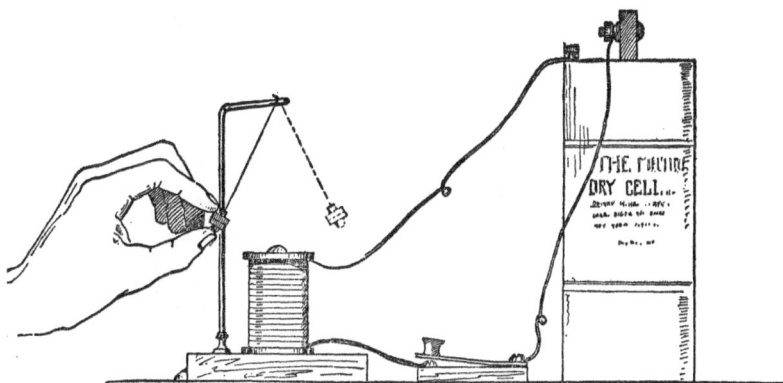

FIG. 81

through it, as shown in Figure 81; suspend over this a steel screw on which you have fastened four or five steel or iron washers or steel nuts. Hold this and let it drop toward the electro-magnet. Place a switch or some other means for breaking your electric current, so that when the pendulum is directly over the circuit, you can open the switch and no current will flow. This will allow the pendulum to pass by to the other side as shown in the dotted lines. When it reaches this position, put the current on again and by a little practice you can keep the pendulum swinging as long as you can get the current flowing. By several automatic means clocks, which are kept running by this principle, have been made.

MAGNETIC INDUCTION THROUGH A GLASS BOTTLE

Place a small quantity of iron filings in a small glass bottle and, by holding any kind of a magnet against the bottle, you will see some very interesting magnetic figures produced.

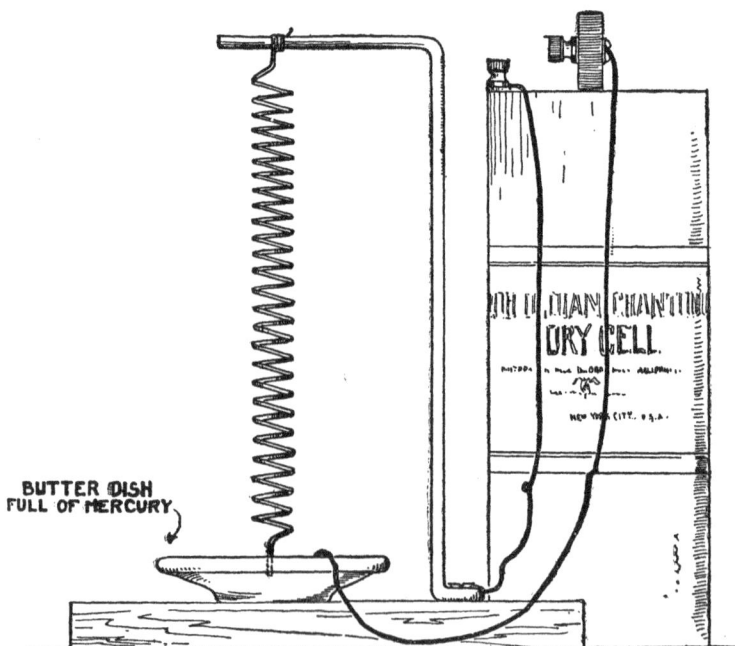

BUTTER DISH
FULL OF MERCURY

FIG. 82

ROGETS SPIRAL

Suspend a coil of bare copper wire, as shown in Figure 82, by means of a brass or iron rod in a block of wood. Make the coil about ⅝ of an inch in diameter, using copper or soft brass wire of about .025 (No. 22 Brown & Sharpe) diameter. Pour a small quantity of mercury or quicksilver into a small butter dish or some similar dish.

Place the dish of mercury under the coil of copper wire in a position so that the bottom end of the coil is touching the mercury. Connect a wire from a battery of 5 or 6 volts with the rod holding the coil and touch the other wire to the mercury. Mercury is a good conductor, so current will flow through the spirals of the coil and the magnetism surrounding the spirals will set up an attraction between the separate spirals. This will cause the spring to contract, and, in doing so, the lower end of the wire will be pulled out of the mercury, causing a break in the circuit and a spark. The weight of the wire and also the spring effect will then send the lower end down again, closing the circuit. When the current flows again, as it will at the closing of the circuit, up jumps the coil end again and so it will go on, up and down, as long as the source of power is connected to the circuit. This experiment is known as Rogets spiral, from the name of the scientist who discovered it.

REPULSION BETWEEN TURNS OF A COIL OF WIRE

In Rogets spiral, we saw the turns of wire attract each other. If you make a coil of wire with some of the coils wound in the opposite direction from the rest—you will find that the coils wound in one direction repel the others when the current is sent through them.

DE LARIVES FLOATING COIL

Figure 83 shows a large cork through which is placed a plate of zinc and another plate of copper. The top of these plates are fastened securely, soldered if possible, to an insulated coil of wire; Nos. 20 to 24 will do for this and fifteen turns should be enough.

Float this device in a small dish of dilute sulphuric acid (or even table vinegar will work). Remember that sulphuric acid can give a very bad burn, so be careful in handling it. You now have a

FIG. 83

wet battery with floating electrodes and a current will flow through the coil of wire. If you now hold a bar magnet near the coil, the latter will be repelled or attracted, depending whether or not the pole of the magnet and the nearest pole of the coil are alike or different. If you thrust the north pole of the bar magnet into the north pole end of the coil, the coil will draw itself off from the bar magnet, float a little way off, and then, turning around, will draw itself on the bar again until it is around the middle of the bar.

HOW TO DE-MAGNETIZE YOUR WATCH

One of the worst things which can happen to your watch is to have it become magnetized. When this happens the different turns of the steel springs are affected and act on each other, causing the watch to keep time poorly. When such a thing happens you can de-magnetize the watch by placing it near an electro-magnet having alternating current for its source of power. A great many jewelers have a solenoid or other form of magnet attached to alternating current circuits, by which they remove magnetism from watches.

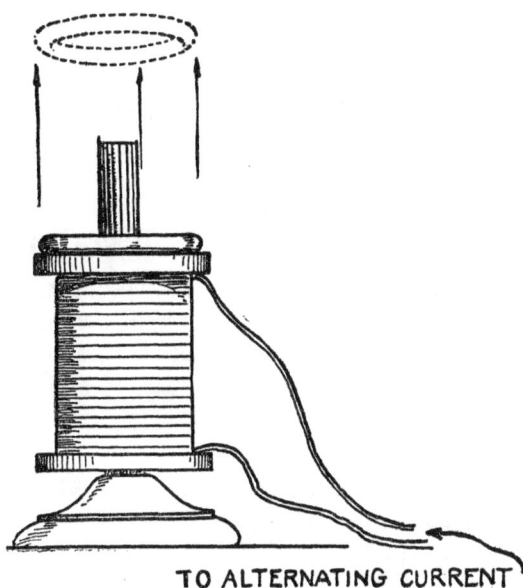

TO ALTERNATING CURRENT

FIG. 84

MAGNET REPULSION
Alternating Current

Make a solenoid and place in it a bundle of iron wires, as shown in Figure 84. Make a ring of thin sheet aluminum which will fit loosely over the iron wire. Connect the coil to an alternating current with a switch, so you can throw the current off and on when you please.

If you place the aluminum ring over the iron wire and then throw on the current, the ring will jump up and attempt to fly off the iron.

This is caused by the fact that the alternating current induces current in the ring, which has a magnetism with it opposing the magnetism of the coil.

In performing this experiment, use a fairly large coil and a light ring. With small coils the power is so small in comparison with the weight of the ring that all the ring will do will be to quiver up and down a very short way, showing that it is trying to move away but is held down by its own weight.

A SIMPLE TELEGRAPH SOUNDER

The telephone and telegraph service depends a great deal for its success on the use of magnets. A study of these magnets would fill a large book. You can make a simple telegraph instrument, however, which will operate on one dry battery and be very good for practice work.

Make a solenoid about 1 inch long and ½ inch in diameter, with a 3/16 inch hole. Wind an insulated copper wire of about No. 22 to No. 26 gauge until ½ inch diameter is reached. Bend a strip of spring brass 1/32 of an inch thick and ½ inch wide in a square form, as shown in Figure 85, and on the end which is underneath fasten a piece of soft iron ½ inch wide and ½ inch long.

Make a key and key knob, as shown in Figure 85. The key should be of spring brass, the knob can be of wood or rubber. To make the sounder work, screw the solenoid and the formed brass arm to a block of wood or fibre in such a way that the round head of the screw comes below the tapped end of the brass arm. Screw the back end of the key through the brass arm to the block. Place a round-headed screw under the knob, the outer end of the sounder key.

Put two terminal posts in the board and on the under side of. the board connect one post to the screw under the knob end of the key and the other to one wire of the solenoid. Fasten the other wire from the solenoid tightly in place under the head of the screw which holds the coil in place. If you now connect a dry battery to the instrument and work the key, you will hear a "click" every time the contacts are closed.

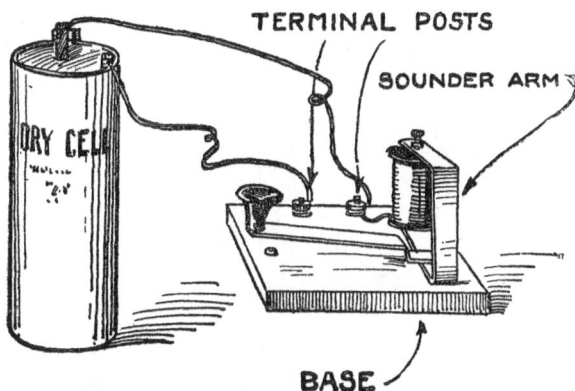

FIG. 85

The screw and nut shown in Figure 85 will improve your instrument very much, as they will adjust the steel tapped arm to the point where the most pull will be given by the magnet and this will make the sharpest sound.

ELECTRIC CLOCKS

Figure 86 shows the principal features required to make the movement for an electric clock.

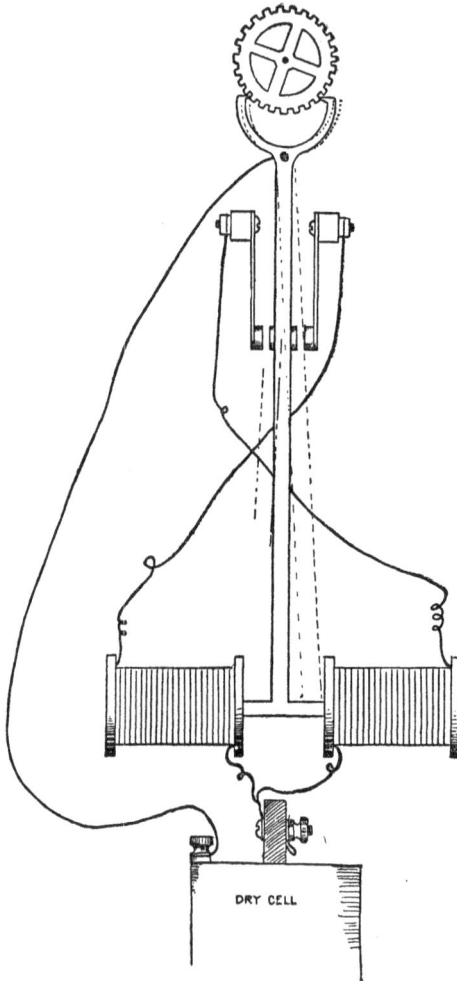

DRY CELL

FIG. 86

The pendulum has two forks at its upper end which alternately push against the teeth of the escapement wheel of the clock. The lower end of the pendulum is T-shaped and each side of the T enters a very loosely fitting electro-magnet. On the shank of the pendulum are maintained two contact points, one on each side. As the pendulum swings, first one, then the other of the contacts is opened and closed. By studying the connection, you will see that these contacts are connected to the magnets in such a way that the iron T of the pendulum is pulled first one way and then the other.

ROTATION OF LIQUIDS

Conducting liquids will show electro-magnetic action. Put a dilute acid or mercury (ordinary table vinegar will also do) into a small tin cup. Connect one wire from a 4 or 6-volt battery to the handle of the cup. Place the second wire so that it just touches the middle of the liquid. Now if you hold the pole of a strong magnet directly over the cup, or rest the cup on the pole of the magnet, the liquid will rotate,

Chapter V

HOW TO MAKE MAGNETS

This chapter is for the boy who likes to work with his head as well as with his hands. It may be a little harder to understand than what is found in the previous chapters, but a mastery of it will give a working knowledge of the design and manufacture of magnets.

PERMANENT MAGNETS

Bar Magnets—Any bar of steel can be magnetized by the methods explained previously, but to get a combination of a strong pull and a permanent quality of the magnetism it has been found best to use special steel.

Dealers in hardware and metals can get this for you from the manufacturers. The manufacturers usually supply the best grade of crucible tungsten steel, which has in it approximately 5 per cent of tungsten, a small amount of the metals chromium and manganese and about .65 per cent carbon. It is interesting to note that our home-made steel of this quality seems equal or better than any of the imported kinds.

A magnet made with this steel will hold the most of its magnetism as long as you will have any use for it.

When you make a bar magnet, select a piece of steel long and thin. It can be either round, square or oblong on the ends. A good proportion of square steel bar for experimental work is 4 inches long; the end dimensions are $\frac{1}{4}$ inch wide x $\frac{1}{4}$ inch high.

If the piece is round and $\frac{1}{4}$ of an inch in diameter, it is suitable. These dimensions are but a suggestion and you can vary them to suit your pleasure.

The next thing to do after you have the steel bar is to harden it. The best way to do this is to take the piece to the blacksmith or a manufacturer who has a steel hardening and tempering room in his factory. Ask him to heat the piece to 850 degrees centigrade, after which he must quench it in pure running water which has a temperature of from 55 to 60 degrees Fahrenheit. If you are unable to have this done for you, you can try hardening it yourself by the following method. Put it in your gas or coal fire and heat it until it turns a bright red. Be sure that the whole piece has turned to the required color. If part of it is dark, it shows that the bar is heated unevenly, and the result will be that the temper will also be unequal. Have a pail of clean water near at hand. When the bar shows the bright red color, take it from the fire with a pair of long-handled tongs; fireplace tongs will do very well.

Plunge the steel bar into the water, but keep hold of it with your tongs. Keep it moving up and down and around in the water until it is cooled down enough so that you can hold it in your hand safely. This should make the bar as hard as glass and very brittle. For ordinary magnets this is what is desired.

For long, thin magnets, which are more than twenty times as long as they are thick, it has been found that a more complicated process is required.

It has long been known that if rods of steel are heated a brilliant red and then quenched, as already mentioned, in water, oil or mercury, they are made very, very hard.

By gently reheating the steel, it will soften a little and turn to a straw color. If still reheated, it will take on a blue shade and also becomes springy and flexible. To be sure of making this long magnet permanent, it should be tempered to either the straw color or the blue.

To any one not familiar with hardening and tempering of steel this process may seem altogether too difficult, and for them it will be much better to buy the magnet steel all hardened rather than try to make it.

The next step is to boil the magnet in water for twenty to thirty hours, after which it is ready to be magnetized. This should be done with an electro-magnet. The writer has seen a very good electro-magnet for this purpose made by using a 5-pound spool of insulated copper wire just as it comes from the manufacturers. For example, a 5-pound spool of No. 19 Brown & Sharpe cotton covered wire can be used. This usually comes on spools about 4 inches high, with ends 5 inches in diameter. The hole through the spool is $\frac{5}{8}$ of an inch in diameter.

To make an electro-magnet of the material mentioned, place a round rod of soft steel or iron in the center hole of the spool, about 6 to 7 inches long, and make it fit tightly in the hole. Clean the ends of the wire and connect them to a direct current source of electricity having a voltage of 90 to 110 volts. Be sure to insulate the joints, connecting the wires of the spool to the outside wire so that you will not short circuit the supply circuit or do any damage to it.

Turn on the current and your magnetizer is ready for use. Touch the end of your steel bar, which is to be made into a magnet, to the end of the soft steel in the center hole of the coil. Leave it there for a minute and then turn off the current. You now have a good permanent bar magnet which will hold its magnetism for a long while. If, however, you want to improve further its lasting quality it will be well to leave it in boiling water for five hours.

If you live near an electrical contractor or dealer in electrical supplies, you can, no doubt, borrow the spool of wire from him long enough to magnetize your bar, since you do not harm or waste any of the wire. Or if you have friends who work in an electrical power house you can get them to touch the bar against a field pole of one of the generators or magnetize it for you in any other of the many ways, which they—the power house men—have at their disposal.

If you are so situated that none of the above methods are at your disposal, you can make an electro-magnet which will operate on 4 dry cells or a 6 volt storage battery, such as used on many automobiles. This will be described under the design of electro-magnets.

HORSESHOE MAGNETS

Horseshoe magnets are simply bar magnets bent into a "U" shape so that the opposite poles are brought near each other. This permits both poles to act on the same piece of metal.

Therefore, to make a horseshoe magnet, or a magnet of any shape other than straight, first heat the steel and bend it into shape. If you desire to put screw holes in it for fastening it to anything, do so after bending. The other operations are then just the same as those used for making the bar magnet.

Remember what was stated in a previous chapter that permanent magnets lose their power if roughly used, so do not hit or throw them about any more than you can help. This is especially true of newly made magnets.

Horseshoe magnets are supplied with a small piece of soft iron or steel called a "Keeper," which is put across the poles when the magnet is not in use. Every time this is slammed against the poles it weakens the magnetism, but it strengthens the magnet to remove the "Keeper" with a sudden jerk.

Keep these points in mind or you may, by carelessly handling your magnet, spoil it and lose all the work you spent in making it.

ELECTRO-MAGNET DESIGN
(SEE FIG. 88)

Before explaining the design of electro-magnets it is necessary that you understand the working principle of current electricity and the standard practice used in making the measurement (see Table B, page 103) of copper wire in addition to the theory of electro-magnets.

(1) **Strength of a Magnet**—This is a term quite different in meaning from lifting power. It is the force of magnetism of one magnet which acts at a distance on other magnets.

(2) **Lifting Power**—The lifting power of a magnet depends on the shape of the magnet and, also, its magnetic strength. A

B — 6

horseshoe magnet will lift three or four times as much as a bar magnet. A long bar magnet can lift more than a short bar magnet, though each is of equal magnetic strength. Curiously enough, a magnet can be loaded to the limit one day and left in that condi-

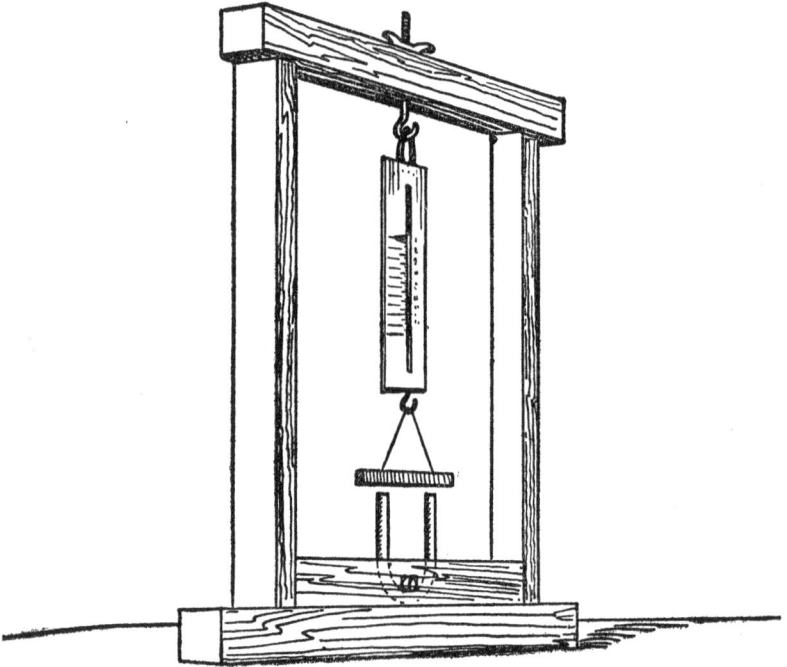

FIG. 87

tion. The next day you will find that you can add a little more to the load, and perhaps for several days you can, little by little, increase the weight until it is considerably larger than what the limit was at the first day.

But if the entire load (often called armature) is torn off, the lifting power at once falls to the limit found on the first day.

If you care to test the lifting power of a magnet, a device similar to that shown in Figure 87 can be used. This shows a magnet fastened securely to a wooden base. From the base is extended an upright, which has a cross bar directly over the top and some distance above the poles of the magnet. Through the cross bar is a screw hook in a hole large enough so that the hook can be moved up or down. The screw end of the hook is extended up through the cross bar, and a thumb nut holds it in place and also is used to adjust the height. Hang a spring balance on the hook and suspend a bar of iron on the balance. Adjust the height of the balance so that the bar is attracted to and touches the poles of the magnet. Now turn the thumb nut until the spring balance is trying to pull the armature (iron bar) away from the magnet; yet the latter has just strength enough to prevent the armature from leaving the poles. Read the pull in pounds as shown on the scale of the balance and you will find the maximum lifting power of the magnet.

The picture shows a horseshoe magnet, but the same method can be used for magnets of any type or form.

ELECTRIC UNITS
Definitions

(3)   Force is the cause of movement—that is pulling or pushing ability.

(4)   Work is Force moved over a distance and is spoken of as foot pounds or inch pounds, which means that a certain number of pounds are moved over a distance measured in inches or feet.

(5)   Power is the completion of a certain amount of work in a given time. Thus, a horsepower is estimated as being equal to 33,000 foot pounds per minute or 550 foot pounds per second.

(6) Electro Motive Force. This is often represented by the letter "E" for the sake of brevity. The practical unit of this force is the volt.

(7) Current. This is the rate at which the electricity passes any point in the circuit and the practical unit is called the ampere, and is represented by the letter "I".

(8) Resistance. Just as water flowing from place to place meets the resistance of rocks, dams, etc., which oppose its flow toward the sea level, so electrical current meets opposition to its flow by many substances.

The unit of practical resistance is called the ohm, which electricians represent by the letter "R." A pressure of 1 volt will push the current of 1 ampere through any circuit which has the resistance of 1 ohm.

From this a celebrated scientist named Ohm made a rule for finding the current in any direct current circuit. The current in amperes (I) equals the volts pressure of the circuit divided by the ohm resistance.

If you want to abbreviate that expression it can be written $I = E \div R$ or $I \times R = E$ or $R = E \div I$.

Example. If you connect a magnet coil having 55 ohms resistance to a house lighting direct current circuit of 110 volts a current will flow which will be $\dfrac{110}{55}$ = 2 amperes.

UNIT OF POWER

The unit of electrical power is called the watt and is equal to 1 volt multiplied by 1 ampere or, to explain it in another way, the power of any direct current circuit is the product of the volts and amperes. 1,000 watts is called a kilowatt. This is abbreviated 1 K.W. 1 K.W. equals about 1 1/3 horsepower.

SHORT CIRCUITS

A short circuit is a condition in which current escapes through breaks in the insulation where it is not intended to go, taking a shorter path than it should. It very often cuts the resistance to a dangerously low value and allows the current to flow in such a quantity that it burns out the conductor.

GROUND

Ground is that condition in electrical circuits when the electricity escapes through some part of the apparatus not intended to be a conductor and is so diverted from its true path.

GENERAL INSTRUCTIONS FOR CONNECTIONS

A few things should be remembered in making experiments with electrical apparatus. Some of them have been mentioned before, but, for the purpose of emphasis, let us run over them again hastily. Remember to treat your permanent magnet with care, as throwing it or banging it tends to weaken its magnetic strength. Where you are using electrical current be sure to make as few joints in the connecting wires as possible. Wherever joints are made, it is necessary to clean the wire until it is bright; for dirt, oil, etc., form good insulators. You can clean the wires by scraping with a knife, file, sandpaper or emery cloth. After you have made these ends clean and bright, fasten them together as closely as possible. If you are making a joint by twisting the wires, make several twists of each wire about the other and, if you can, then solder the joint, especially if the winding is to be permanent. If you are placing the ends of the wire under a screw or binding nut, twist the part around the screw; then fasten the screw or binding nut down as firmly as possible, remembering that a loose joint or poorly soldered wire increases the resistance of your circuit, therefore cutting down the strength of your current.

AMPERE TURNS

This is an expression used by electricians which means the total number of turns in any coil multiplied by the amperes flowing through it.

Example. If you have a coil of 300 turns through which $\frac{1}{2}$ an ampere of current is flowing, the result in ampere turns equals $300 \times \frac{1}{2} = 150$. The abbreviation for ampere turn is A.T.

CONDUCTORS AND RESISTORS

A material which offers little opposition to the flow of electrical current is called a conductor. Materials which strongly resist the movement of the amperes are called resistors.

The following list gives the names of materials in the order of their resistance, starting with the lowest resistance and going on toward the highest:

1. Silver	14. Manila Paper
2. Copper	15. Cotton
3. Gold	16. Silk
4. Aluminum	17. Paraffin
5. Zinc	18. Beeswax
6. Brass	19. Resin
7. Iron	20. Ebonite
8. Nickel	21. Gutta Percha
9. Tin	22. Shellac
10. Steel	23. Glass, ordinary
11. Lead	24. Mica
12. German Silver	25. Porcelain
13. Dry Air	26. Flint Glass

From this list you can see that the cheapest and best conducting material is copper. This is used for almost all electrical work, though aluminum and iron are also used, but in very small quantities compared to copper.

The most convenient way found was to draw the copper into a wire. In order to wind it in small space, the different coils are separated from each other by a high resistance material called an insulator.

The four most common insulators for copper wire are cotton, silk, rubber and enamel. Cotton and silk thread is wrapped around the wire. The rubber and enamel is coated on the wire. All these are good insulators and keep the current flowing where it is intended to go.

The cotton and silk are put on both as a single covering and also a double covering. In choosing the insulations, the main thing to consider is the space it takes up, as you may have but little room in which to wind the required amount of wire.

COPPER WIRE

Copper wire is made in many sizes. The standard practice now is to list these sizes according to the Brown & Sharpe gauge, known as the B & S gauge.

A list of the sizes giving the outside diameter of the wire, bare and also insulated, is very useful. A list of the most useful sizes will be found on page 102, Table A.

Table B is also a very useful table, giving the largest number of turns it is possible to wind in a square inch of space.

DESIGN OF AN ELECTRO-MAGNET

Now let us design a magnet for lifting a block of iron, keeping in mind what was stated previously, that the holding force of a magnet, and this applies to an electro-magnet, depends not alone on its magnetic strength but on the shape of the poles. It also depends somewhat on the form of the material which we want to make it attract, and because of the form of the metal to be lifted as well as the shape of the poles, it is not possible to make a set of rules which will be quite true for all conditions. The following rules are very good and have been in use for many years. They are true and exact when all conditions are of the best, such as those we would have for a long magnet of comparatively small pole force area, lifting a smooth soft iron block having clean flat surfaces and offering a short magnetic path to the lines of magnetic force.

In magnets under actual working conditions, we do not find many of these good qualities and so the usual practice is to design and build our magnets in accordance with the following rules: After the coils are in place connect them with a current which can be varied and measured. Send a current through the coils of such a strength that the magnet will lift the required weight. You then can read the number of amperes flowing; and knowing the number of turns on the coil, you then multiply the number of turns by the number of these amperes and the proper ampere turns will then be found.

The rule for such a magnet is: The pounds weight to be lifted is equal to the square of the density multiplied by the area of the pole face in square inches and this product is divided by 72,134,000.

The abbreviation of this rule is shown

$$P = \frac{B \times B \times A}{72,134,000} \tag{1}$$

P = Pounds weight.

B = Density in magnetic lines per square inch.

A = Area of the pole face in square inches.

Formula (1) can be rearranged in various ways as follows: When the weight to be lifted and the area of the core pole piece is known it is

$$(B \times B) = \frac{P \times 72,134,000}{A} \tag{2}$$

or, if the weight and the magnetic density is known, to find the area of the pole force the formula should read

$$A = \frac{P \times 72,134,000}{B \times B} \qquad (3)$$

By density we mean the number of magnetic lines passing through each square inch of the iron core of the electro-magnet.

If you use cast iron for this core, the density used should not be *over* 35,000 lines per square inch; for cast steel use 95,000 or less; and for cold rolled steel or sheet steel 100,000 lines per square inch.

Suppose we want to make an electro-magnet for use with a 6-volt battery.

Such a battery is used on many automobiles or you can make one for experimental work, where it is to be used a short time only, by connecting 4 dry batteries together in series—that is, in such a way that the outside binding post of one is connected to the inside post of the next and so on.

Imagine that this magnet will not be required to lift more than 50 pounds. Then we will make the soft steel or yoke of a "U" shaped, round, cold rolled steel rod bending it to shape.

Since we are using this horseshoe shaped yoke, the load will be carried on two poles or, in other words, each pole will carry one-half the load or 25 pounds.

From the foregoing rule, we find the following example to solve: one pole to lift 25 pounds; then the area of the pole face—that is, the area of the round end which touches the weight—to be lifted is equal to 25 multiplied by 72,134,000 and this result divided by the density $B \times B = (B)^2$. We are using cold rolled steel, so let us choose a density of 95,000 magnetic lines or slightly less than our limit of 100,000. Then 95,000 x 95,000 = 9,000,000,000.

(In dealing with such large numbers the first one or two figures only, need be exact.)   If you multiply the above, you find that the exact answer is 9,025,000,000.

Now our rule reads

$$A = \frac{25 \times 72,134,000}{9,000,000}$$

Solving this example we get an answer

$$\frac{1,800,000}{9,000,000} = .2 \text{ sq. in.}$$

The area of a circle is equal to the diameter multiplied by itself, that result multiplied by 3.1416, and the answer divided by 4.

$$A = \frac{3.1416 \times D^2}{4}$$

In Table E, on page 106, you will find a list of areas and circumferences for circles having diameter from $\frac{1}{64}$ of an inch to 10 inches.

Looking at this table, we find that the nearest diameter for an area of .2 is $\frac{1}{2}$ inch, with an area of .1963 sq. in.

Since we did not use the highest limit of magnetic density, we can afford to have our steel area just a little smaller than called for in the rule.   If you solve the area formula, you will find the exact diameter required is .504 inches.

Let us make our yoke in "U" form using a 2-inch rod, $6\frac{1}{4}$ inches long.   Bend this so that the legs are parallel and $1\frac{3}{8}$ inches apart.

AMPERE TURNS REQUIRED

We now have a steel rod $6\frac{1}{4}$ inches long, through which magnetic lines of force are to be pushed at the rate of 95,000 per square inch (density). From Table C, on page 104, we find that for every inch of length our metal at 95,000 lines is, we must have 47 ampere turns. Since we have 6¼ inches, our total number of ampere turns will be at least

$$6.25$$
$$\underline{47}$$
$$4375$$
$$\underline{2500}$$
$$293.75 \quad \text{call it 294}$$

Before we decide on how many turns and what size wire we will use, let us first make a spool for holding the wire. This must slip on over the yoke and, therefore, the hole in it must be a little over ½ inch in diameter.

Cut a piece of tin can, or better yet a piece of sheet brass. The thickness should be about .012 of an inch. Cut two pieces 1⅝ inches wide and 1¾ inches long. Slit the ends in four or six places, spaced equally apart at each end. Make the slits ⅛ of an inch deep.

Roll the pieces into the form of a tube, with the ends touching, not lapping. The length of the tube should be 1¾ inches and the hole through it a little larger than ½ inch. Smooth off all rough spots and edges with a file.

Cut two strips of paper, ordinary letter paper will do, make it 1½ inches wide and long enough to wrap around the metal until the outside measures ⅝ of an inch. Wrap each tube with a paper and glue the outside end of each paper down, leaving ⅛ of an inch sticking out from each side of the paper.

Make four circular discs of heavy cardboard or fibre. These should have a hole in the center so they will be a tight fit over the end of the metal tubes. The outside diameter of these discs should not be more than 1 ⁹⁄₁₆ inches. The thickness should be about ¹⁄₁₆ of an inch.

It will help if you make little holes in each fibre, one near the inside and another near the outside edges, through which the ends of the wire can be pushed. Force these fibre discs on each end of the metal tube until they press tightly against the ends of paper wrapper. Lock them in place by turning up the ends of the tube where they are slit and hammer the turned up metal as lightly as possible against the fibre washers. When this is done, we have two spools on which we will wind our wire. The winding space is 1½ inches long, leaving a little of the fibre washer standing out above the winding. The wire may be laid in layers until it is ⅜ of an inch deep (⅜″ = .375″).

RULES FOR FINDING TURNS AND WIRE SIZE

Size wire in circular mils is equal to the diameter of the wire in inches multiplied by itself.

Circular Mils = Ampere turns multiplied by 1.03, and multiply this by the number of poles to be used for lifting. Divide this result by the volts supplied, then this answer must be multiplied by the mean length of turn.

The mean length of turns is the average length in inches of each turn of the winding and for abbreviation we call it M.L.T.

M.L.T. = the sum of the circumference of the tube, including insulating paper on which the coil is wound and 3.1416 multiplied by the depth of the winding.

The formula is M.L.T. = C + 3.1416D.

C = Circumference of tube,

D = Winding depth,

and the formula for circular mils then can be written

$$\text{Cir. M.} = \frac{\text{AT} \times 1.03 \times \text{No. of poles}}{6} \times \text{M. L. T.}$$

Example.   First we will find the circumference of the tube formed by the paper insulation.

Our steel core is $\frac{1}{2}'' = .5''$ in diameter, our metal tube wrapping around it on each side is .012 inches thick; that gives us a diameter of

$$
\begin{array}{r}
.500 \\
.012 \\
.012 \\
\hline
.524
\end{array}
$$

then the paper builds this up to about .625. From Table D, on page 105, we find this equals $\frac{5}{8}$ of an inch. Table E, page 106, shows the circumference for this diameter is equal to 1.9635. We find the depth we will divide by to be $\frac{3}{8}$ of an inch = .375 inches. $3.1416 \times .375 = 1.1781.$

$$
\begin{array}{r}
1.9635 = C \\
1.1781 = D \times 3,1416 \\
\hline
3.1416 = \text{M.L.T.}
\end{array}
$$

AT POLES

$$
\frac{294 \times 1.03 \times 2}{6} = 100.94
$$

$$
\begin{array}{r}
3.1416 \\
60564 \\
10094 \\
40376 \\
10094 \\
30282 \\
\hline
317.113104 \text{ circular mils, use 318.}
\end{array}
$$

Looking in Table A, page 102, we find that No. 25 wire has 320.4 circular mils and this is the nearest size to what we want. In choosing the wire, use the size which will be a little larger than required, if there is no wire exactly suitable to the size your example requires.

So we know that we may use No. 25 wire, but first we must find out whether or not the current in flowing through the wire of this size will heat the coil too much. It has been found that if we figure the watts given off in relation to the square inches of outside surface of the winding, we can determine a safe value for heating. For magnets in use all the time—that is, in continuous duty—the watts per square inch should not be more than .7.

For magnets in use only a few minutes at a time—that is, intermittent duty—our value can be 2.8 or less.

For magnets for very short time of work—that is, momentary duty—the value can be as high as 11.2.

The rule to find this value is: first find the value AT ÷ winding space and this answer multiplied by itself. Let us call this

$$\left(\frac{AT}{W.S.}\right)^2$$

Then our complete rule is: **Watts per square inch surface** =

$$\frac{\left(\frac{AT}{W.S.}\right)^2 \times .78 \times M.L.T.}{\textbf{Depth} \times \textbf{Space factor}} \times \textbf{M.L.T.} + \textbf{3.1416} \times \textbf{depth} \times \textbf{1,000,000}$$

This means: $\left(\frac{AT}{W.S.}\right)^2$ multiplied by .78, this result by the mean length of turn. This we will call Answer No. 1. Also, multiply the winding depth by the space factor, this result by the sum of the mean length of turn and 3.1416 times the winding depth, and this result by 1,000,000. This we will call Answer No. 2.

Space Factor. In this formula you find the space factor. This is a value which represents the decimal part of the winding space actually occupied by the bare copper. For example, if in Table B, we see that 2630 turns of enamel wire, size No. 25, can be wound in one square inch, but 2630 turns of bare, No. 25, have a cross section of only

$$
\begin{array}{r}
.000254 \\
2630 \\
\hline
7620 \\
1524 \\
508 \\
\hline
.668020
\end{array}
$$

Cross section in inches = circular mils × .785 × .000001. A mil = .001 inches and a square mil = .00001 of a square inch, that is, .668 of a square inch, then .668 ÷ 1 = .668 or the ratio of the bare copper in the winding space to the winding space.

Table B values are for coils wound evenly row on row. It is very seldom that coils are wound as carefully as this so it is usual to use a space factor lower than what is shown in the table. A good plan will be to subtract .1 from the value found for all irregular wound coils.

Now we can attempt to work our problem. Let us call our space factor .57.

$$\text{Watts} = \frac{\left(\frac{2.94}{1.5}\right)^2 \times .78 \times 3.157}{.375 \times .57 \times 4.345 \times 1,000,000}$$

$$
\begin{array}{r}
1.5\,)\,\overline{294}\,(\,196 \\
15 \\
\hline
144 \\
135 \\
\hline
90 \\
90 \\
\end{array}
$$
  (A)

$$
\begin{array}{r}
196 \\
196 \\
\hline
1176 \\
1764 \\
196 \\
\hline
38416 \\
\end{array}
$$
  (B)

$$
\begin{array}{r}
38416 \\
.78 \\
\hline
307328 \\
268912 \\
\hline
29964.48 \\
\end{array}
$$
  (C)

```
      29964 .48                                      (D)
          3 .157
      ─────────
      20975136
      14982240
       2996448
       8989344
      ─────────
      94597 .86336    Answer No. 1.

           .375
            .57
         ────────
          2625
          1875
         ────────
          .21375                                     (E)
         4 .345
        ─────────
        106875
         85500
         64125
         85500
        ─────────
        .92874375                                    (F)
       1000000
      ──────────
      928743 .75    call it 930000    Answer No. 2.  (G)
```

Dividing Answer No. 1 by No. 2 we have

```
      930000 ) 94597 .86336 ( .1017 +
               930000
              ────────
               1597863
                930000
              ────────
               6678633
               6510000
              ────────
                168633
```

This shows we have a safe beating, and we can now determine the number of turns of wire per coil.

RULES FOR TURNS PER COIL

Multiply width of winding by the depth and the result by the space factor. Divide this answer by the area of the wire cross section in square inches; you will have the turns required.

$$\text{Turns} = \frac{\text{width} \times \text{depth} \times \text{space factor}}{\text{Area of wire section}}$$

Example. Our winding space is 1.5 inches, the depth .375 inches, the activity .57, and the area of our wire = .000254 inches.

$$\text{Turns} = \frac{1.5 \times .375 \times .57}{.000254} =$$

```
       1 .5
        .375
        ----
         75
        105
         45
        -----
        .5625
          .57
        -----
        39375
        28125
        -------
        .320625
```

```
.000254 ) .320625 ( 1262 +    call it 1263
          254
          ----
          666
          508
          -----
          1582
          1524
          -----
           585
           508
           ---
            77
```

Then we will wind our coils with 1263 turns of enameled copper wire, size No. 25.

Let us prove our figures to be sure of them. If our M.L.T. is 3.1416 inches, our total number of turns have a length of

B — 7

1263 turns.

$$3.1416$$

$$\begin{array}{r} 7578 \\ 1263 \\ 5052 \\ 1263 \\ \hline 3789 \end{array}$$

12) 3967 .8408 inches (330 .65 ft.　call it 331.

$$\begin{array}{r} 36 \\ \hline 36 \\ 36 \\ \hline 078 \end{array}$$

The resistance per ft., see Table A = .03231.

$$\begin{array}{r} 331 \\ .03231 \\ \hline 331 \\ 993 \\ 662 \\ 993 \\ \hline \end{array}$$

10 .69461 ohms.　call it 10 .7 ohms.

We are to connect two coils together in series so our total resistance = 21.4 ohms. We must multiply this resistance by 1.15 to allow for the fact that after heating a well designed copper coil will increase its resistance at about this value

$$\begin{array}{r} 21.4 \\ 1.15 \\ \hline 1070 \\ 214 \\ 214 \\ \hline \end{array}$$

24 .610 ohms hot.

$$\text{Amperes flowing} = \frac{6 \text{ volts}}{24.6} = .244 \text{ amperes}$$

$$\begin{array}{r}
\textbf{1263 turns} \\
\textbf{.244 amperes} \\
\hline
\textbf{5052} \\
\textbf{5052} \\
\textbf{2526} \\
\hline
\textbf{308.172 ampere turns}
\end{array}$$

Our required number is 294, so we show a difference in our favor of 14 ampere turns.

Now we can put our coils on the magnet yoke. Fasten them in place by wrapping some sticking-tape around the steel just on each side of the fibre washer. Let the ends of the wire be brought out at least a foot from the coil so you can make the necessary connections.

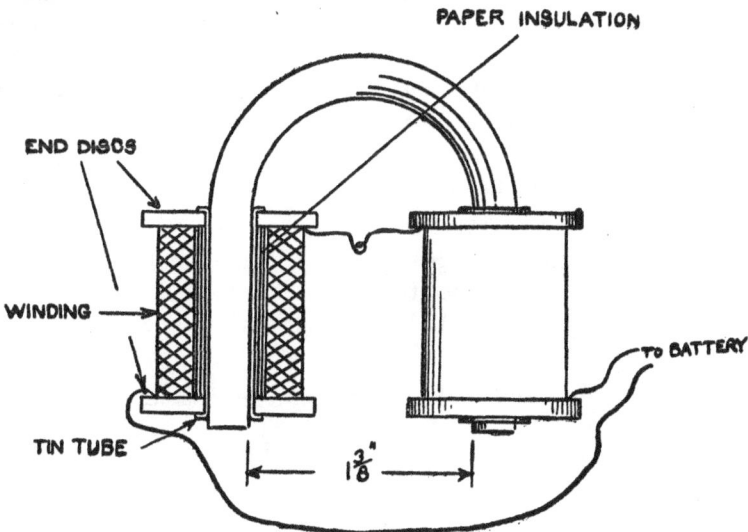

FIG. 88

Figure 88 shows one of these coils split in half to show the paper insulation and the other details of construction. This is close enough for all practical purposes and these rules have been used many times to design magnets.

MOVING CORE MAGNETS

Moving core or plunger magnets are of the type which pull or suck their core up into them. The magnetic guns described in the chapter on magnetic toys and tricks is one of these. In the circuit breaker, also, the pull exerted on the moving core, is quite different from that of a lifting magnet.

The magnetizing force of a solenoid is greatest at its center and only about one-half of the full value at the ends. That fact causes the soft iron core, or plunger as it is often called, to become magnetized and sucked into the hole in the solenoid. As the plunger passes along, it becomes more and more filled with magnetic lines by induction until it becomes saturated. If it is not much longer than the solenoid winding, the pulling effect stops when the magnetic centers of the coil and core are in the same place. From this you will see that the greatest pull comes just after the plunger has passed the middle point of the coil, except for some very long coils and also some very short ones.

The rules for these plunger magnets are somewhat more complicated than are those for the lifting magnet, so we will not give them here, but a few points may be mentioned which will help in planning such a magnet.

Make your coil with a diameter about three times its diameter if possible. The length of the pull is in proportion to the coil length. Make your core at least one and one-half times the length of the coil.

To increase the pull, a short fixed core can be placed in the end opposite to that which the plunger is to enter.

POLARIZED MAGNETS

An electro-magnet pulls its armature one way even though the current in the coil is reversed.   But if the armature is made of a permanent magnet in place of the usual soft iron and is placed between the poles of the electro-magnet instead of in front of them, the direction in which it is moved can be changed by changing the direction of current flowing in the coils.

EXPLANATIONS FOR TABLE A

A mil = 1/1000 of an inch.
A circular mil = diameter of the wire in mils × itself.
S.C.C. = Single cotton cover.
D.C.C. = Double cotton cover.
Enam. = Enameled.

Table A

B&S	Copper Wire Outside Diameter						Circular Mils	Foot per lb.	Ohms per ft.
	Bare	Enam.	S.C.C.	D.C.C.	Single Silk	Double Silk			
1	0.2893			0.303			83690	3.947	0.0001237
2	0.2576			0.272			66370	4.977	0.000156
3	0.2294			0.242			52630	6.276	0.0001967
4	0.2043			0.216			41740	7.914	0.000248
5	0.1819		.189	0.194			33100	9.98	0.0003128
6	0.1620		.169	0.174			26250	12.58	0.0003944
7	0.1443		.151	0.156			20820	15.87	0.0004973
8	0.1285	.1306	.1355	0.1416			16510	20.01	0.0006271
9	0.1144	.1165	.1214	0.1274			13090	25.23	0.0007908
10	0.1019	.1040	.1079	0.1129			10380	31.82	0.0009972
11	0.09074	.0927	.0967	.1017			8234	40.12	.001257
12	.08081	.0828	.0868	.0918			6530	50.59	0.0001586
13	.07196	.0704	.078	.083			5178	63.79	.001999
14	.0648	.0661	.0701	.0751			4107	80.44	0.002521
15	.05707	.0591	.0631	.0681			3257	101.4	0.003179
16	.05082	.0528	.0558	.0608	.0528	.0546	2583	127.9	.004009
17	.04526	.0470	.0503	.0553	.0473	.0491	2048	161.3	.005055
18	.0403	.0421	.0453	.0503	.0423	.0441	1624	203.4	.006374
19	.03589	.0377	.0400	.0459	.0379	.0397	1288	256.5	.008038
20	.03196	.0337	.0370	.0420	.0340	.0358	1022	323.4	.01014
21	.02846	.0302	.0335	.0385	.0305	.0323	810.1	407.8	.01278
22	.02535	.0269	.0293	.0333	.0273	.0291	642.4	514.2	.01612
23	.02257	.0241	.0261	.0306	.0246	.0264	509.5	648.4	.02032
24	.02010	.0215	.0241	.0281	.0221	.0239	404.0	817.6	.02563
25	.01790	.0192	.0219	.0259	.0199	.0217	320.4	1031	.03231
26	.01594	.0171	.0199	.0239	.0179	.0197	254.1	1300	.04075
27	.0142	.0153	.0182	.0222	.0162	.0180	201.5	1639	.05138
28	.01264	.0136	.0166	.0206	.0146	.0164	159.8	2067	.06479
29	.01126	.0122	.0153	.0193	.0133	.0151	126.7	2607	.08170
30	.01003	.0109	.0140	.0180	.0120	.0138	100.5	3287	.1030
31	.008928	.0097	.0129	.0169	.0109	.0127	79.70	4145	.1299
32	.007950	.0087	.01195	.01595	.00995	.01175	63.21	5227	.1638
33	.007080	.0077	.01108	.01508	.00908	.01088	50.13	6591	.2066
34	.006305	.0069	.01030	.01430	.00830	.0101	39.75	8311	.2605
35	.005615	.0062	.00961	.01361	.00761	.00941	31.52	10480	.3284
36	.0050	.0055	.00900	.01300	.00700	.00880	25.0	13210	.4142
37	.004453	.0049	.00845	.01245	.00645	.00825	19.83	16660	.5222
38	.003965	.0044	.00796	.01196	.00596	.00776	15.72	21010	.6585
39	.003531	.0039	.00753	.01153	.00553	.00733	12.47	26500	.8304
40	.003145	.0035	.00714	.01114	.00514	.00694	9.888	33410	1.047

Table B

TURNS PER SQUARE INCH

B & S	Beld-Enamel	Single Cotton	Double Cotton	Single Silk	Double Silk
8	57	53	48		
9	72	66	59		
10	90	84	76		
11	113	104	93		
12	141	129	114		
13	177	160	140		
14	221	198	171		
15	277	245	208		
16	348	312	260	351	327
17	437	383	316	437	405
18	548	472	378	548	503
19	681	581	455	682	619
20	852	712	545	848	761
21	1065	868	650	1055	935
22	1340	1128	865	1315	1150
23	1665	1370	1030	1620	1400
24	2100	1665	1215	2010	1705
25	2630	2020	1420	2470	2070
26	3320	2445	1690	3005	2510
27	4145	2925	1945	3680	3010
28	5250	3500	2250	4600	3620
29	6510	4120	2560	5530	4270
30	8175	4900	2930	6810	5100
31	10200	5770	3330	8260	6010
32	12650	6700	3720	9870	6990
33	16200	7780	4140	11850	8160
34	19950	9010	4595	14250	9480
35	25000	10300	5070	16800	10870
36	31700	11750	5550	19850	12430
37	39600	13250	6045	23300	14100
38	49100	14900	6510	27300	15960
39	62600	16600	6935	31700	17850
40	77600	18400	7450	36700	19900

Table C
AMPERE TURNS AND MAGNETIC DENSITY

CAST IRON		CAST STEEL		COLD ROLLED STEEL		ANNEALED SHT. IRON	
Mag. Density B	Amp. Turns per In.	Mag. Density B	Amp. Turns per In.	Mag. Density B	Amp. Turns per In.	Mag. Density B	Amp. Turns per In.
20000	23	20000	7	20000	6	20000	3
25000	31	25000	7	25000	6	25000	3
30000	44	30000	8	30000	7	30000	3
35000	61	35000	9	35000	8	35000	4
40000	87	40000	9.5	40000	8	40000	4
45000	Cast Iron Highly Satu-rated with Density above 40000	45000	10	45000	8.5	45000	4
50000		50000	11	50000	10	50000	5
55000		55000	13	55000	11	55000	6
60000		60000	15.5	60000	13	60000	8
65000		65000	17.5	65000	15	65000	10
70000		70000	21	70000	17	70000	13
75000		75000	25.5	75000	21	75000	16
80000		80000	31	80000	25	80000	20
85000		85000	38	85000	30	85000	25
90000		90000	50	90000	38	90000	33
95000		95000	70	95000	47	95000	42
100000		100000	110	100000	61	100000	59

Table D

DECIMAL EQUIVALENTS OF ONE INCH

1/64	.015625	17/32	.53125
1/32	.03125	35/64	.546875
3/64	.046875	9/16	.5625
1/16	.0625	37/64	.578125
5/64	.078125	19/32	.5937
3/32	.09375	39/64	.609375
7/64	.109375	5/8	.625
1/8	.125	41/64	.640625
9/64	.140625	21/32	.65625
5/32	.15625	43/64	.671875
11/64	.171875	11/16	.6875
3/16	.1875	45/64	.703125
13/64	.203125	23/32	.71875
7/32	.21875	47/64	.734375
15/64	.234375	3/4	.75
1/4	.25	49/64	.765625
17/64	.265625	25/32	.78125
9/32	.28125	51/64	.796875
19/64	.296875	13/16	.8125
5/16	.3125	53/64	.828125
21/64	.328125	27/32	.84375
11/32	.34375	55/64	.859375
3/8	.375	7/8	.875
25/64	.390625	57/64	.890625
13/32	.40625	29/32	.90625
27/64	.421875	59/64	.921875
7/16	.4375	15/16	.9375
29/64	.453125	61/64	.953125
15/32	.46875	31/32	.96875
31/64	.484375	63/64	.984375
1/2	.5	1	1.
33/64	.515625		

Table E
CIRCUMFERENCES AND AREAS OF CIRCLES

Diam.	Circum.	Area in Sq. Ins.	Diam.	Circum.	Area in Sq. Ins.
1/64	.0491	.0002	4 1/2	14.1372	15.9043
1/32	.0982	.0008	4 5/8	14.5299	16.8002
1/16	.1963	.0031	4 3/4	14.9226	17.7206
1/8	.3927	.0123	4 7/8	15.3153	18.6555
3/16	.5890	.0276	5	15.7080	19.6350
1/4	.7854	.0491	5 1/8	16.1007	20.6290
5/16	.9817	.0767	5 1/4	16.4934	21.6476
3/8	1.1781	.1104	5 3/8	16.8861	22.6907
7/16	1.3744	.1503	5 1/2	17.2788	23.7583
1/2	1.5708	.1963	5 5/8	17.6715	24.8505
9/16	1.7671	.2485	5 3/4	18.0642	25.9673
5/8	1.9635	.3068	5 7/8	18.4569	27.1086
11/16	2.1598	.3712	6	18.8496	28.2744
3/4	2.3562	.4418	6 1/8	19.2423	29.4648
13/16	2.5525	.5185	6 1/4	19.6350	30.6797
7/8	2.7489	.6013	6 3/8	20.0277	31.9191
15/16	2.9452	.6903	6 1/2	20.4204	33.1831
1	3.1416	.7854	6 5/8	20.8131	34.4717
1 1/8	3.5343	.9940	6 3/4	21.2058	35.7848
1 1/4	3.9270	1.2272	6 7/8	21.5985	37.1224
1 3/8	4.3197	1.4849	7	21.9912	38.4846
1 1/2	4.7124	1.7671	7 1/8	22.3839	39.8713
1 5/8	5.1051	2.0739	7 1/4	22.7766	41.2826
1 3/4	5.4978	2.4053	7 3/8	23.1693	42.7184
1 7/8	5.8905	2.7612	7 1/2	23.5620	44.1787
2	6.2832	3.1416	7 5/8	23.9547	45.6636
2 1/8	6.6759	3.5466	7 3/4	24.3474	47.1731
2 1/4	7.0686	3.9761	7 7/8	24.7401	48.7071
2 3/8	7.4613	4.4301	8	25.1328	50.2656
2 1/2	7.8540	4.9087	8 1/8	25.5255	51.8487
2 5/8	8.2467	5.4119	8 1/4	25.9182	53.4563
2 3/4	8.6394	5.9396	8 3/8	26.3109	55.0884
2 7/8	9.0321	6.4918	8 1/2	26.7036	56.7451
3	9.4248	7.0686	8 5/8	27.0963	58.4264
3 1/8	9.8175	7.6699	8 3/4	27.4890	60.1322
3 1/4	10.2102	8.2958	8 7/8	27.8817	61.8625
3 3/8	10.6029	8.9462	9	28.2744	63.6174
3 1/2	10.9956	9.6211	9 1/8	28.6671	65.3968
3 5/8	11.3883	10.3206	9 1/4	29.0598	67.2008
3 3/4	11.7810	11.0447	9 3/8	29.4525	69.0293
3 7/8	12.1737	11.7933	9 1/2	29.8452	70.8823
4	12.5664	12.5664	9 5/8	30.2379	72.7599
4 1/8	12.9591	13.3641	9 3/4	30.6306	74.6621
4 1/4	13.3518	14.1863	9 7/8	31.0233	76.589
4 3/8	13.7445	15.0330	10	31.4160	78.540

MEMORANDUM

MEMORANDUM

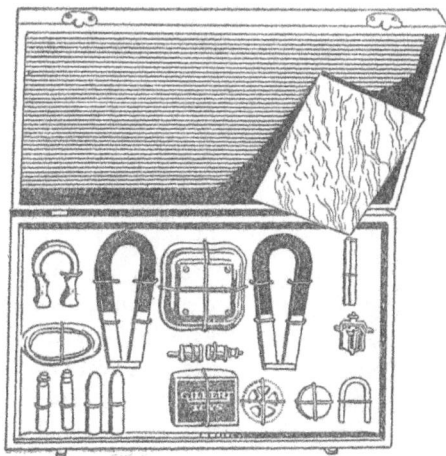

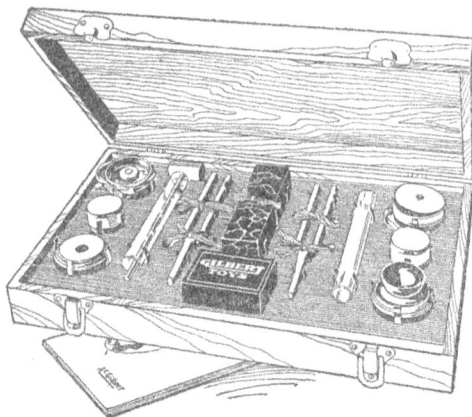

WHAT IS SOUND?

Do you know that hearing is just feeling with the ear? That in reality, the thing we call sound, which we think of as a noise or as a musical note, is just an impression on the brain? Very few boys know this, and if you would like to be one of the few that do, you surely want an outfit of

Gilbert
Sound Experiments

With one of these outfits you can find out just what sound is — how it is produced — why some pianos sound better than others — why a violin produces a musical tone, and many other things, including a number of startling table rapping tricks with which you can astonish your friends. A big book of instructions tells you how to perform every experiment. Get one of these outfits today. The best toy dealer in your town should have it; if not, write us and we'll tell you where you can get it.

THE A. C. GILBERT COMPANY
509 BLATCHLEY AVE. NEW HAVEN, CONN.

In Canada: The A. C. Gilbert-Menzies Co., Limited, Toronto
In England: The A. C. Gilbert Co., 125 High Holborn, London, W. C. 2

Boy Carpenters

You will find a Gilbert Tool Chest a most valuable home accessory. It will save its cost many times over each year. With it you can do a great many handy things about the house — build yourself useful and attractive pieces of furniture.

Tool Chests with Real Tools

Every tool in a Gilbert Tool Chest is a real tool — the kind a carpenter would buy for his own use. The steel is finely tempered and each tool is perfectly finished. They are the kind real workmen want. In each chest is the book "Gilbert Carpentry," that tells you how to do various kinds of work — how to get the best results.

There are Gilbert Tool Chests to fit every need from the smaller chests containing an assortment of small tools to the very complete outfits with the highest grade tools packed in the special Pershing Expeditionary Outfit Chest.

Gilbert Tool Chests are on sale at all good dealers. If unable to find the one you want, write us.

THE A. C. GILBERT COMPANY
New Haven, Conn.

In Canada: The A. C. Gilbert-Menzies Co., Limited, Toronto
In England: The A. C. Gilbert Company, 125 High Holborn, London, W. C. 1

www.ingramcontent.com/pod-product-compliance
Lightning Source LLC
LaVergne TN
LVHW011211080426
835508LV00007B/720